OTHER NOVELS BY KEVIN HENKES

The Year of Billy Miller
Junonia
Bird Lake Moon
Olive's Ocean
The Birthday Room
Sun & Spoon
Protecting Marie
Words of Stone
The Zebra Wall
Two Under Par
Return to Sender

SWEEPING
UP THE
HEART

KEVIN HENKES

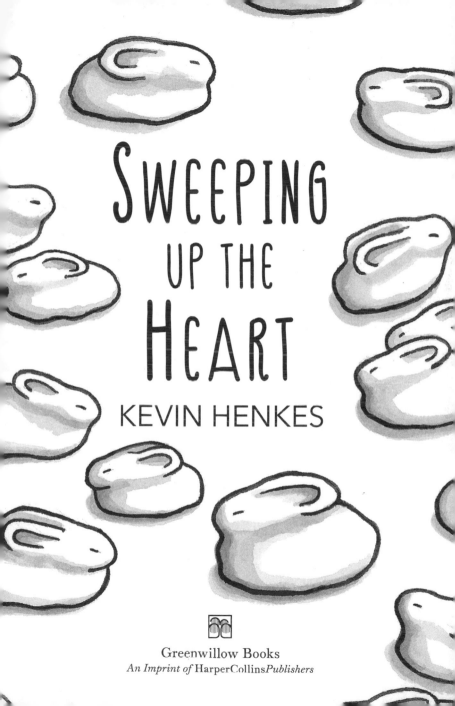

Greenwillow Books
An Imprint of HarperCollins*Publishers*

Sweeping Up the Heart

Copyright © 2019 by Kevin Henkes

The Emily Dickinson poems on pages 48 and 50 are taken from THE POEMS OF EMILY DICKINSON, edited by Thomas H. Johnson, Cambridge, Mass.: The Belknap Press of Harvard University Press, Copyright © 1951, 1955 by the President and Fellows of Harvard College. Copyright © renewed 1979, 1983 by the President and Fellows of Harvard College. Copyright © 1914, 1918, 1919, 1924, 1929, 1930, 1932, 1935, 1937, 1942, by Martha Dickinson Bianchi. Copyright © 1952, 1957, 1958, 1963, 1965, by Mary L. Hampson. This was the standard edition of Dickinson's poems in 1999, when this novel takes place.

The text of this book is set in 11-point Monticello LT Roman.
This book is printed on acid-free paper.

Library of Congress Cataloging-in-Publication Data

Names: Henkes, Kevin, author.
Title: Sweeping up the heart / Kevin Henkes.
Description: First edition. | New York, NY :
Greenwillow Books, an imprint of HarperCollinsPublishers, [2019] |
Summary: "After an eventful spring break, seventh-grader
Amelia Albright's life changes forever"—Provided by publisher.
Identifiers: LCCN 2018022067|
ISBN 9780062852540 (trade ed.) | ISBN 9780062852557 (lib. bdg.)
Subjects: | CYAC: Friendship—Fiction. | Sculptors—Fiction. |
Single-parent families—Fiction. | Fathers and daughters—Fiction. |
Dating (Social customs)—Fiction.
Classification: LCC PZ7.H389 Swe 2019 |
DDC [Fic]—dc23
LC record available at https://lccn.loc.gov/2018022067

19 20 21 22 23 PC/LSCH 10 9 8 7 6 5 4 3 2 1
First Edition

Greenwillow Books

For Clara

The whole secret is something
very few people ever discover.

—William Maxwell, *The Heavenly Tenants*

1 · POOR THING

Poor Amelia Albright.

Gordon Albright's daughter.

Poor thing, people said.

It was Mrs. O'Brien who said it most often. Nearly every day.

Right now Amelia couldn't agree more with the sentiment. Poor me, she thought. It was the beginning of spring break. Saturday. She should have been happy, excited to be free of the curse of seventh grade for a week, but she felt a nagging disappointment in general, and sharp pinpricks of anger specifically directed toward her father.

She'd begged him for months to take her

on a trip during break. Rarely did her vacation and his fall upon the same dates. When she'd discovered that they did, in fact, coincide this year, her vision became crystal, and she'd begun her campaign for a trip to Florida. It seemed everyone at school was going to Florida, a place she'd never been. The other place she wanted to go was France, to visit her friend who was living there for a year, but she didn't dare suggest it; his going along with *that* idea seemed as unlikely as her mother showing up at the front door.

"Florida?" her father had said, the word placed gently, but like a roadblock, between them. "Too hot."

"Too crowded," he'd said later.

"Too touristy," he'd said later still.

He'd barely mentioned the drawing of the seashell or the ceramic dolphin she'd made and left at the door to his study.

The last time she'd asked him, he'd pursed his lips thoughtfully, then said, "You know I don't like to travel." He sighed his typical sigh, then added in his typically measured voice, "We'll have a nice quiet time at home."

"That's all I ever have," said Amelia. "That's my life—a nice quiet time at home. Minus the 'nice.'"

He looked her firmly in the eye. His gaze was sympathetic, but weighty. "It could be worse. I do the best I can."

At that point she walked out of the room, knowing it was a lost cause. She didn't want to hear it. She'd heard it too many times before. He'd say that he understood how hard it was for her. But that it was just as hard if not harder for him. How do you argue with that? Although she could never do it, one day she thought she might like to scream at him, "Get over it!"

When Amelia Albright was two years old, her mother died of cancer. She didn't remember her mother at all. The only life she knew was her life with her melancholy father and Mrs. O'Brien.

2 · MRS. O'BRIEN

Mrs. O'Brien moved around the kitchen like a leaf in the wind. With a quick bouncing step, she went from the cupboard to the refrigerator to the counter to the table. She served Amelia a homemade bran muffin, a bowl of strawberries, and a glass of chocolate milk.

"What will the day hold for you?" asked Mrs. O'Brien.

"Well, I won't be getting a suntan on the beach," said Amelia.

"I know," said Mrs. O'Brien. "I know." She kissed the air above Amelia's head. "Poor thing."

Amelia ate without speaking. She picked apart the warm muffin with her fingers, then ate the pieces with a fork. No surprise: the muffin was delicious, but Amelia kept her compliments to herself. Nothing against Mrs. O'Brien. Amelia's mood was to blame for her silence.

Mrs. O'Brien was busy at the sink with her back to Amelia. She was an expert at gauging Amelia's frame of mind. She knew when to probe and when to leave her alone.

As usual, Mrs. O'Brien was wearing what Amelia thought of as her uniform: tan sweatpants, puffy white shoes that reminded Amelia of marshmallows, a baggy short-sleeved men's polo shirt in a pastel color, and her pearl necklace. Her hair was the shape and color of a mushroom cap.

Mrs. O'Brien seemed ageless. She looked the same as she did when she first came to cook and clean ten years ago. It was an interesting arrangement. Mrs. O'Brien lived across the street, but she was at the Albrights' every day. As reliable as the sun, she arrived before Amelia got up in the morning. And she didn't leave until Amelia had gone to bed at night.

"Where's the Professor?" Amelia asked suddenly.

Mrs. O'Brien turned from the sink toward Amelia. Sunlight caught the side of her face, making her look ethereal. "Your father's at his office on campus. He left early."

Amelia rolled her eyes. "It figures," she said. "Who else would be working during break? And, it's *Saturday*."

"Now, now."

"I mean, it would be one thing if he were curing some disease or ending world hunger. But he's probably just sitting at his messy desk in his dark office reading Jane Austen or *The*

Canterbury Tales for the five hundredth time. For *fun!*" she added bitterly.

Mrs. O'Brien laughed. She approached Amelia and touched her lightly on her arm, gave a gentle squeeze. She left her hand there for an extra moment as if to absorb all bad feelings. "I do wish Natalie were home."

"Me, too."

Natalie Vandermeer was Amelia's best friend. She was gone for the whole school year. The Vandermeers were living in France and wouldn't be back until August. Amelia missed Natalie terribly. At first they stayed in touch regularly with postcards and letters sent back and forth. But as the weeks and months passed, their communication was less and less frequent. She hoped they were still best friends.

"What would lift your spirits?" asked Mrs. O'Brien.

Amelia shrugged. She knew that she could

make any request and Mrs. O'Brien would try her best to fulfill it. Mrs. O'Brien was the adult in her life who made her feel most safe, most cared for. Amelia wore Mrs. O'Brien's loving watchfulness like a protective cloak. "I'm going to the clay studio. Hopefully that'll lift my spirits."

"When will you be home?"

"I don't know. I'll call you."

"What about lunch?"

"I'll figure it out. The Professor gave me money yesterday."

Amelia finished breakfast quickly, put her dishes in the sink, threw on her jacket, slung her backpack over her shoulder, yelled goodbye, and was out the door.

"Make something pretty for me," called Mrs. O'Brien.

3 · KNOBBY KNEES

The clay studio was Amelia's second home, especially with Natalie away. It was only five blocks from her house, in the middle of a row of small, neat, brick-faced shops that also included a grocery, a coffee shop, an antique store, a florist's, and a dry-cleaning business.

Amelia had been introduced to the studio when she was six. Her father had enrolled her in an after-school program. Something clicked the very first day of that very first class. From the moment she plunged her fingers into the squishy gray blob placed before her and began forming a pinch pot for Mrs. O'Brien, she was hooked.

Afterward she pleaded with her father to let her take any and every available class, and he was happy to oblige her. Although she learned how to use the potter's wheel and throw fairly accomplished bowls and vases, what she came to love best was building small pieces by hand, animals of all kinds: birds, rabbits, elephants, whales. And so, lately, that's what she'd been doing nearly every day after school and on Saturdays. Her growing menagerie seemed to multiply spontaneously. She kept it in her bedroom and on bookshelves and windowsills throughout the house.

Amelia covered the short distance at a clip, an oddly rhythmic clip. She was moving quickly because she was eager to work, but more to the point she was reinventing her walk, trying to make it faster and more graceful. Purposeful. Her legs had grown so much lately that she felt out of sync, as if her body belonged to someone or something else. And she'd recently decided that she hated her knees. They were big and knobby. Like a camel's. She was skipping, or something close to it, when she tripped on the curb. She didn't fall and no one was around to see her, but she could feel her face redden nonetheless. She slowed down and tried not to think about walking.

It was early April. The low cement skies of winter had lifted, but it was still chilly, cold even—a far cry from how she pictured Florida. Something about the weather put her in a wistful mood. She slipped into thinking about her mother. She had no memory of her. Nothing. Nothing lay curled in her mind; there was nothing to draw up and remember. Her father rarely talked about her; neither did Mrs. O'Brien. When Amelia thought of her mother, images from a few photographs were what she saw in her head, and what she experienced was a general, mild loneliness. Can you be lonely for someone you never knew?

A car backing out of a driveway honked, startling her. Then she wondered about herself—something she was doing a lot lately. She wondered about her own place in the world. What would it be? Who would she become? Would she stay in Madison, Wisconsin, all her life? Or would she travel widely and move far away?

She wondered why she, Amelia Epiphany Albright, often felt so unlike everyone else. She wondered when her real life—the one she'd been waiting for—would finally begin.

It was 1999. Where would she be in a year? In ten? In less than nine months it would be 2000. All the numbers in the year would be changing. That seemed important to Amelia. Maybe, soon, something important will happen to me, she thought.

She wondered if knowing her mother would have provided answers to all that was unsolved within her. And then she wondered if her mother had had knobby knees, too.

All of it—life, the world, her knees—was so strange if you thought about it long enough. And whenever she felt like she understood even a tiny piece of the world, the understanding disappeared right away like a light shutting off.

A sudden gust of steely wind brought her attention back to the present. She considered what animal she might make today. And, once again, she concentrated on her walk, picking up her pace, doing a combination trot-shuffle the rest of the way.

1 · THE NEPHEW

Amelia sensed that something was different the minute she opened the door. She walked through the front of the clay studio—the part that was a gallery—and straight back to the workroom. She was right—something was different. Louise Kirkwood, the owner, was nowhere in sight, and sitting in Amelia's favorite place at the table in the far corner was a boy.

The boy was wearing headphones. He was hunched over a sketchbook, but he wasn't drawing. He was drumming out a rhythm with a pencil, eyes closed, one pinkie hooked in the corner of his mouth, his head jerking about to the beat of whatever he was listening to. His hair was a thick dark tumble. His curls bounced as he moved.

Seeing someone in her spot caused a dropping sensation in Amelia's chest. From across the room she cleared her throat.

No response.

She came closer, tugging the collar of her jacket.

Nothing.

She tucked a strand of her long gingery hair behind her ear and bit her lower lip. She snapped the rubber band around her wrist.

When the boy finally saw her, he froze, giving her a long look. Then he yanked off the headphones and stood, scraping his chair on the floor. "You must be Amelia," he said, blushing. He blinked as if he were waking from a nap or emerging from water. "My aunt, Louise, said you might be coming."

Besides his impressive hair, Amelia took note of his pale, perfect skin and his blue, blue eyes. The other thing that caught her attention was his shirt: a gray T-shirt with a big white wedding cake on it. There was something written on the cake, but she couldn't make out the letters, and she didn't want to stare.

The boy, noticing her glance, looked downward and said, "Oh, I made it—the shirt. Long story." Then he sat again.

That was it for a moment. Neither spoke. The introduction was left awkwardly unfinished.

Amelia's throat tightened with disappointment. She had envisioned this morning differently. She had seen herself blissfully alone (except for Louise) at her usual spot, absorbed in her work. And now she was faced with the nephew in the wedding cake shirt, hogging the table with his enormous sketchbook and several large photography and art books opened to pictures of the Eiffel Tower. Why the Eiffel Tower? "Where *is* Louise?" she asked, her voice oddly pitched.

"Right here."

Amelia turned around to see Louise bracketed by the doorframe for a second before she stepped into the workroom. Louise's entrance was a bright spot in what was already a not-so-bright day. It was the suddenness of the entrance that made it all the brighter.

"Breakfast," said Louise, smiling. With one hand she raised a bag from the coffee shop down the street; her other hand held a Styrofoam cup with a plastic lid. Her round, welcoming face was vivid from the crisp air. When she crossed the room to her desk in the back, Amelia could smell the lovely, sugary smell of bakery. Louise set down the bag and took a sip from her cup. "So you've met—yes?"

After a pause, Amelia said, "Not really."

"Sort of," said the boy.

"All right," said Louise. "Amelia Albright, meet my nephew, Casey Kirkwood-Cole." A kindly smile. "And, Casey—this is Amelia." Louise nodded to each. "Casey's staying with me all week. So he'll be here—working, making art, keeping me company. . . ." She gave him a significant look, eyes widening, a look Amelia thought was full of love and sadness. "And— you're both *twelve*," she added with a little too much exuberance, as if this had just occurred to her and was particularly meaningful.

Casey cocked his head slightly—a kind of shrug.

Amelia tried to hide her feelings. She hugged herself. Her expectations for the day— the week!—had crumbled. "Hi," she managed to say.

Casey said, "Hey," and motioned with his

hand, his pencil/drumstick laced between his fingers.

"I got doughnuts at the coffee shop," said Louise. "Who's hungry?"

"I am," said Casey, perking up, rubbing his hands together like a fly, having stuck his pencil into his mass of hair.

It—this morning—wasn't what she'd planned on, that was certain, but it was what it was. She had nowhere to go, nothing else to do. She'd stay. She'd already shrugged off her jacket and scoped out a new place to work at another table. She really wasn't hungry, but in an effort to turn the day around, she lied. "Me, too."

5 · RABBIT

Amelia stared at the lump of clay for about a hundred years. And then she forgot it was a lump of clay and she pushed and pulled and pinched and poked. She smoothed and carved and smoothed. She concentrated. She smashed it flat and began again.

What started out being a slender deer turned into a long-necked bird and then a squat rabbit with ears like paddles. The rabbit was good. She liked it. She gave it eyes and a tail.

She'd forgotten about Casey Kirkwood-Cole and Florida. She'd entered a space of her own making—a bubble—and was lost in a private reverie. It was strange—the rabbit was a real thing now and she was part of it and it was part of her. Fully absorbed, she watched it, watched her fingers reshape and shift things— the tail, the nose—ever so slightly. And then she felt as if she were the one being watched.

Casey.

"You're good," he said.

"Thanks."

"*Really* good."

She felt the bubble thin to nothing. She was back—alone with Casey.

Amelia turned her head, scanning the room. She wondered where Louise was. She'd been in the background all morning—flitting in and out of Amelia's awareness like music— preparing for an afternoon class for little kids on the other side of the workroom, mixing big buckets of glaze, and making trips to the basement to unload and load the kiln.

Casey rose and walked over to Amelia. He bent down to get a better look at her rabbit. "Aunt Louise said you were a good artist," he told her, nodding.

"I'm okay."

"Yours is much better than mine," said Casey. "I'll show you."

Amelia followed him reluctantly back to his work area, thinking it was the polite thing to do.

"Ta-da," said Casey, gesturing with his open hands, hamming it up ironically.

They stared at his creation. It was kind of a mess. Amelia was at a loss for words.

"I'm better at drawing than I am with clay," Casey explained.

Amelia rubbed her chin with the back of her wrist, her brain whirring, trying to come up with something to say that wouldn't offend him but that wasn't a lie, either.

"It's supposed to be the Eiffel Tower," Casey

said with a doubtful expression. "But it kept collapsing so I kept making it smaller. Now it stands up okay, but it's so small and crooked it looks like—like the skeleton of a miniature giraffe with really bad arthritis."

Casey's comment had the effect of opening a window in a stuffy room. Amelia laughed. And then so did Casey.

They were still laughing when Louise came up from the basement carrying a tray of children's coil pots fresh from the kiln and ready for glazing. "What's so funny?" she asked.

Amelia and Casey quieted, exchanged a look—and burst out laughing again. Then they got the giggles.

"Oh, good," said Louise, amused. She breezed past them, glancing from one to the other. "I thought you might hit it off."

6 · GWEN AND CHARLIE TILL DEATH DO US PART

The day had changed. When Amelia had set out for the clay studio the sky had been muted, nearly invisible, and now it was as blue and bright as a gemstone. But it was still cold. Amelia turned up the collar of her jacket and dipped her chin even though they only had a block to walk.

Louise had given money to Casey for lunch at the coffee shop. "Here," she'd said, pressing some folded bills into his hand, "this is for both of you. My treat."

On the way, Casey managed to brush his arm against Amelia's arm two times. Amelia

couldn't decide if this was annoying or interesting. Or accidental.

If you didn't know the two of them, and
were walking behind them at a close distance,
you might even think they liked each other.

They ordered at the counter, Amelia first,
and sat on stools at the high, long communal
table against the window, facing the street.
When their food arrived—a grilled cheese
sandwich and hot chocolate for both—Casey
grinned and said, "Just so you know, I wasn't
copying you." For the most part, while they ate,
they looked out the window, not at each other.

Amelia's questions about Casey were adding
up. Why was he staying with Louise? Why
was he trying to make a replica of the Eiffel
Tower? And what was with the wedding cake
shirt? She'd stolen enough glances throughout
the morning to read the words on the cake.
The words said *Gwen and Charlie Till Death*

Do Us Part. Who were Gwen and Charlie?

Gwen and Charlie Till Death Do Us Part could be the name of an alternative band or a cult movie. Amelia wasn't very knowledgeable about things like that. She was not on the cutting edge. She still had a Protect Our Ocean Friends poster hanging above her bed.

After swallowing a bite of her sandwich, she jumped right in. "Is Gwen and Charlie Till Death Do Us Part a band?"

Casey laughed. "No." His eyes strayed to his shirt. "That's funny. Gwen and Charlie are my parents."

"Oh," said Amelia. "Did they just have an anniversary or renew their vows, or something?"

"I wish. Actually, they're thinking about getting divorced." Casey folded his napkin into a triangle. "They went on some marriage retreat at a resort in Michigan. That's where they are right now. I overheard my mom, on the phone, before they left, say it's their last attempt to fix their failing marriage. That's why I'm staying with my aunt. Louise is my mom's sister."

Amelia didn't know how to respond. She nodded and frowned.

"My dad told me that their marriage is a shipwreck," said Casey.

"That's bad," said Amelia. "Really sad."

"But, he's also been known to say that *life* is a *universal* shipwreck. He's a cheery guy."

Out of the corner of her eye Amelia watched Casey. He held up what was left of his sandwich and studied it as if it were a specimen in science class. She noticed that he'd somehow gotten a big crumb—a piece of bread crust—caught in his wild hair. She wanted to pick it out or tell him, but she didn't dare.

"I think it's probably hopeless," he said, "but . . ." He didn't finish. He twisted his mouth, then puffed out his cheeks. "Anyway, I started making these shirts with fabric markers and acrylic paint. My 'Save the Marriage' campaign. This one—the cake—is my favorite. I have one that says *For Better or Worse*. And another that says *Children of Divorce Are More Likely to Drop Out, Do Drugs, Commit Crimes.* My mom hates that one. *Really* hates it."

"Is that true?" Amelia asked cautiously. "What the shirt says."

He shrugged. "I don't know. I just made it up. My mom says it's not true."

Casey jammed the rest of his sandwich into his mouth and covered his mouth while he chewed. He appeared to be talking to his hand or telling a secret.

He sat back and chewed, slowly, thoughtfully, for a long time. When he was done, he leaned in. "They met at the Eiffel Tower when they were in college," he explained. "That's why I'm trying to make one—an Eiffel Tower."

He rolled his eyes. "Dumb, I know."

"No, it's not."

"You don't think it's weird?"

"No. It's nice."

"How's *your* parents' marriage?" asked Casey.

The question caught Amelia off guard and hung between them for a long moment.

"What about your parents?" Casey pressed on. "Are they divorced? Statistically, it's almost normal."

"No, they're not divorced."

"You're lucky."

She waited a beat, then as casually as possible, said, "My mom's dead."

"Oh." His face reddened. His neck, too. "That's—that's—" He was obviously flustered. "I'm sorry. I'm really sorry."

"It's okay. I was only two when she died. I don't even remember her."

As sometimes happened, Amelia's statement shut down the conversation like a door slamming. Amelia thought that if Casey were an adult, this is when he'd say, "Poor thing." They both stared out the window. They finished eating without speaking.

Casey's next question pierced the silence. "Do you ever get signs from her?"

Another surprising question. She looked right at him. "No," she said. No, she never got signs. None that she was aware of, anyway. Then she looked out the window again. Cars and people passed by in both directions, in and out of the shadows, like fish in an aquarium. Her eyes hopped from a crying baby in a stroller to a jogger with glaring orange shoes to a poster on an idling bus advertising an art exhibit downtown. Behind it all, above it all, between the branches, the sky was blue. Nothing unusual.

A sign.

A sign.

What would a sign look like? she wondered.

7 · FEATHER

Amelia was still looking out the window wondering about a sign from her mother when she saw Lindy Tussler. How could she miss her? Lindy edged along the window, then nearly pressed her face against the glass. She was using the window as a mirror, canting her head and fluffing her purple-streaked bangs. She seemed to be admiring her reflection when all at once, she saw Amelia, recognized her, and contorted her face into an expression of pure disgust. Then she mouthed the word *freak*.

Amelia drew back and stiffened.

Lindy lifted her chin and turned away. Amelia watched her catch up with Connor Gup, who was waiting for her. Hand in hand they walked off.

"Who was that?" asked Casey. He crinkled his nose. "Do you know her?"

"She goes to my school."

"Is she a monster? Or does she just appear to be one?"

Amelia chuckled, but her ears burned. "Monster."

And she was. But she hadn't always been that way.

"We used to be friends when we were little," said Amelia.

"Really? What happened?"

Amelia shrugged. "I don't know. At the start of fifth grade, we kind of drifted apart. She started hanging around with a different group." She dumped me, is what Amelia was thinking. "She turned mean." It was one of the many sad mysteries of life.

Amelia remembered the moment it happened with burning clarity. They were walking through the cafeteria during the first week of fifth grade. For two days they'd been sitting together for lunch at the table with other kids who weren't part of a large group. Kids alone or with one other kid. Loose ends. Leftovers. As they neared their table, Shelby Granger called Lindy over to her noisy, bustling one. Amelia could still hear Shelby's voice, high and sure, circling inside her head like a bird: "Hey, Lindy. Sit here." And Lindy turned on her heel and let herself be drawn to Shelby as if she'd lost all control over her body. That was it. Amelia was left standing alone like a single tree on a cartoon desert island. There was no "Goodbye." No "Come with me." No "See you later." No "Sorry." Nothing. It confused Amelia then. Still did. Although, now, she tried not to care.

Natalie Vandermeer had been at the other table, and when Amelia, eyes shiny with tears, joined her, sitting next to her, Natalie pushed a chocolate chip cookie in front of her. "Here," she said quietly, looking off to the side. And she and Amelia sat together from that day on. Day by day their shyness disappeared and their friendship grew.

Casey shifted urgently on his stool. "Do you ever make up stories for people?" he asked, craning his neck, catching a final glimpse of Lindy and Connor.

"What do you mean?"

"You know, personal histories. Take your former friend and that guy she's with. We could give them names and make up stories for them."

"I already know their names. Hers is Lindy Tussler. He's Connor Gup."

Casey shook his head. "We can do better than that." He grinned, apparently delighted by the possibilities. Amelia could tell he was thinking hard by the way he narrowed his eyes and chewed his lower lip. "Okay," he said, after a moment, "her name is Feather."

"Feather?"

"Yeah. And no last name. Like Madonna or Prince." He nodded. "Feather."

Amelia laughed. "She's the opposite of a feather." Lindy was big-boned and fairly tall and kind of loud.

"That's what makes it good," said Casey. "*And*—her story is that she collects salt and pepper shakers in the shapes of barnyard animals. She has hundreds." He paused.

"Lots of pigs," said Amelia suddenly, surprising herself. "*Mostly* pigs."

Casey continued gleefully. "She spends her weekends going to rummage sales and antique shops, adding to her collection," he said. "It's an obsession."

Amelia laughed again. "And marshmallow Peeps are her favorite food. She has them hidden all over her house, and she binges on them." She was enjoying this. It seemed justified. Harmless payback for past heartbreak.

Casey took a deep breath and exhaled loudly. "Now, what about her friend?"

Amelia ran her thumb up and down the handle of her mug. She didn't know much about Connor Gup. He was undeniably cute. He played soccer. He was popular. Someone who lived and breathed in a world unlike hers. She was not in his orbit, not even close.

"Let's call him Ronnie Wayne Valentine," said Casey. "He always wears boxer shorts with hearts on them. Pink boxers with red hearts."

"And," said Amelia, eager to add something, "he has a heart tattoo that says *I love myself*."

"On his *butt*," said Casey, his voice rising, relishing this last contribution. "Oh, and best of all, he's still a member of the official Lego fan club." He smiled, pleased, and Amelia noticed that his smile was uneven, curving up on one side more than the other.

Their game wound down and they sat quietly, hunched forward, elbows on the table, heads bent slightly toward each other. Amelia experienced a feeling of being included, of being part of something with someone her own age, something she hadn't felt since Natalie had left for France. A shift in the sunlight falling across the tabletop underscored the change inside her.

Suddenly Louise filled the window, her arms outstretched, her hands open, her fingers splayed. Her eyes got as big as coins, then she pointed to her watch. Her gestures and expression were easily interpreted: *Are you coming back? What's taking so long?*

"Oh!" said Casey, jumping up. "I forgot, I said I'd help with a kids' class." He rushed off.

Amelia slipped down from her stool. She scurried, following Casey to the entrance. As she moved through the tables, she struggled into her jacket.

"Let's do this again," said Casey, in flight, over his shoulder.

"Okay."

At the door, he turned around, facing her. "I mean, making up stories for people. Well, and having lunch, too."

"Yes and yes," said Amelia.

8 • DR. COTTON

The rest of her day at the clay studio passed quickly, as if someone had taken the hands on the big clock above the door and spun them around a few times. A children's class had come and gone, Amelia had made another rabbit, and then, before she knew it, she was walking home in the late, dim afternoon carrying the promise of meeting Casey again on Monday.

That night, in bed, Amelia felt particularly happy—and content and something else. Something more. Something hard to put into words. Now the coming week had shape to it. Maybe her real life was finally beginning.

After her eyes had adjusted to the darkness, she could see Dr. Cotton on the shelf across the room. Dr. Cotton was a stuffed lamb with black plastic glasses, whom she'd had all her life. When she was little, he was her security object and went everywhere she did. Over the years he'd grown drab and limp and pilly, and now he stayed put, but she couldn't bear to get rid of him.

She'd named him Dr. Cotton because, back then, he was white and soft and looked as if cotton balls had been sewn all over his body.

"Wouldn't Dr. *Wool* be a more fitting name?" her father had asked repeatedly.

At the time she had no idea what her father was getting at, and so she ignored his suggestion and he eventually stopped asking.

More than once Mrs. O'Brien had told her, "I think Dr. Cotton is a lovely name."

Although she didn't need him the way she

used to, Dr. Cotton was still important. She talked to him sometimes—usually in her head, usually in bed, right before she got up in the morning or when she was trying to fall asleep. She imagined him answering in a sweet, low voice. She talked to him the way she supposed some people talked to God.

Oh, Dr. Cotton, you wouldn't believe what happened at school. . . .

Dear Dr. Cotton, let me do well on my history test. . . .

Please, Dr. Cotton, make the Professor be in a good mood today. . . .

That night, her interior monologue began, *Well, Dr. Cotton, it was a very interesting day. . . .* She went on to tell him about Casey and Lindy, the remembered moments making their way into the catalog of her life. And then she stopped addressing Dr. Cotton and simply let her mind drift, one thought leading to the next. From the Eiffel Tower to France to Natalie. Wearily, she pulled the covers up to her chin and adjusted her pillow. Her thoughts had a rhythm to them, like music. Eventually, the music slowed and dragged and froze. She'd fallen asleep.

Happy.

9 · POETRY GROUP

Early Sunday morning Amelia was pulled from bed by a wave of good smells. She hurried downstairs, not fully herself yet, and stubbed her toe on the kitchen threshold, making a clumsy entrance.

Mrs. O'Brien rushed forward, steadying Amelia with an oddly graceful hug. "Careful," she said.

Amelia closed her eyes and surrendered to the embrace. "Ouch," she whispered. "Ouch, ouch, ouch."

"Poor thing," said Mrs. O'Brien. "I know that hurts."

Amelia let her head rest against Mrs. O'Brien's shoulder until the dull pain was gone. It struck her that she'd soon be taller than Mrs. O'Brien, and for some reason, the thought made her sad. "Do I smell coffee cake?" she asked, stepping back, hoping.

Mrs. O'Brien nodded. "And there'll be date scones and blueberry muffins, too. Today's my poetry group."

Amelia smiled. The meeting of Mrs. O'Brien's monthly poetry group meant delicious food and lots of it. The group always met at Amelia's home, because as Mrs. O'Brien explained, everyone loved discussing poetry in the home of an English professor, surrounded by bookshelves crammed with important books.

And, if by some chance, the group caught a glimpse of Gordon Albright, Ph.D., or even better, he offered an opinion of or a biographical tidbit about the current poet of the month, well, the group (eight women in their seventies) was beside itself with joy.

"Come," said Mrs. O'Brien. "You have to look at something. Before it's gone." She steered Amelia to the window above the sink where the sky was streaked with pink and orange, colors as bright as sherbet.

"Pretty," said Amelia.

"Isn't it?" said Mrs. O'Brien. "So lovely." She took Amelia's hand and squeezed it until it hurt.

"Perfection," said Amelia's father, who'd appeared out of nowhere, startling them both. With his usual stiffness, he put one hand on Amelia's shoulder and the other on Mrs. O'Brien's. The three of them stood there, gazing out the window. "They don't make skies like this in Florida," he said evenly.

Of course, they do, thought Amelia, but she didn't say a word. Her father couldn't get the best of her today. She was still happy from the day before, content with the world. At that moment, she loved everyone.

Mrs. O'Brien's mouth was pursed as if to speak; she remained silent, but she looked right at Amelia, dismissing the Professor's comment with a flick of her hand. Then she said, "I'll make the two of you a beautiful breakfast."

And she did.

Afterward Amelia helped Mrs. O'Brien prepare for the guests to arrive. She stacked plates, folded napkins, and set out mugs. She arranged slices of coffee cake on a platter. She filled one basket with scones and another with muffins.

The guests—Mrs. O'Brien's friends—would always fuss over Amelia as soon as they showed up. They'd coo about her sculptures; they'd ask her what she was reading; they'd admire her "pretty red hair." It was as if each of them was one of her many grandmothers and she was the favorite grandchild.

Funny, Amelia felt more at home with these perfumy, friendly old women than she did with girls her own age. Was that strange?

When the food was ready, Amelia looked through the books Mrs. O'Brien had spread out on the coffee table. Emily Dickinson was the poet to be discussed. Mrs. O'Brien had put together a mini-library—there were biographies, books of poems, even a few children's books. Some of the books had Post-it notes marking certain pages. Amelia picked up a well-worn paperback that had several Post-it notes sticking out of it.

Earlier that school year, Amelia had studied Emily Dickinson in Ms. Noggle's English class. Amelia had memorized the poem that began, "I'm Nobody! Who are you? / Are you–Nobody–Too?"

She'd so identified with that poem, and when she'd learned of Emily Dickinson's introverted, reclusive life, and of her eccentric tendency to wear only white dresses, her fondness for her deepened. She felt she understood her. She even imagined that if by some trick of time they'd been classmates, they would have been friends.

At one point in class, Lindy Tussler had raised her hand and said, "I think Emily Dickinson was a freak. Simple as that."

"No she's not!" said Amelia, without thinking. "She's brilliant!"

"You two would have been a perfect couple," said Lindy, lowering her voice. "A freaky, weirdo couple."

Everyone within earshot laughed.

Amelia was grateful that Ms. Noggle hadn't heard.

Now Amelia burned inside, remembering the incident. Her eyes were glittering, and she was sure her cheeks and ears were red.

Amelia turned her attention back to the book in her hands. She glanced at the poems Mrs. O'Brien had flagged. The first line of one of the poems was "The Bustle in a House." The Post-it marking it had writing on it. In Mrs. O'Brien's familiar, neat, petite cursive, it said *Reminds me of Gordon, explains him.*

Because of Mrs. O'Brien's note, Amelia read the poem hungrily.

The Bustle in a House
The Morning after Death
Is solemnest of industries
Enacted upon Earth–

The Sweeping up the Heart
And putting Love away
We shall not want to use again
Until Eternity.

Amelia read the poem three times. She pictured her father's heart literally broken into tiny pieces. She pictured Mrs. O'Brien sweeping up the pieces and putting them into a jar, her hollowed-out father watching with a grave, faraway look in his eyes. She pictured the jar stashed away on some high shadowed shelf—in her father's bedroom closet or in his study or in his office on campus.

Amelia knew her father loved her on a basic level, but maybe this poem explained his inability to express his love in an easy, natural, common way. Maybe, because of her mother's death, he couldn't love, really love, anyone or anything ever again.

Amelia shivered. She closed the book with a snap. She wished she hadn't read the poem.

10 · QUIZ

And, then, finally, it was Monday morning. Amelia felt steady inside as she entered the clay studio. There was a glimmer of light in her dull life.

She could see Casey in the workroom. He was busy writing in a notebook. His head was inclined, his hand and arm moved jerkily, in spurts, up and down, back and forth. Beside him, drying, stood a new Eiffel Tower. Tall. Elegant. Beautiful.

"Wow," said Amelia, instead of a greeting. "That's really good."

"Well," said Casey, waving the compliment

away, "Louise helped a lot." He flashed an off-kilter grin. "Actually, it's more hers than mine."

Amelia circled the sculpture, looking closer. "When did you make it?"

"Yesterday."

"What happened to the other one?"

"I smashed it into a million pieces," said Casey. "That was fun."

Amelia couldn't tell if she was jealous of the new Eiffel Tower or not. It was really good. "What are you going to work on today?" she asked.

"I'm working on this," he replied, tipping his head toward his notebook.

"What is it?"

"I'm writing a quiz about myself for my parents to take. They've both been so caught up in hating each other that I feel like they don't really know me anymore. So, I'm hoping that taking the quiz—which I'm sure they'll both fail—will shock them into staying together. For my sake, if nothing else." He looked up at her with his heart in his eyes.

"Maybe they know more than you think they do."

"I doubt it. I'd even be willing to be direct and say, *If you pass the quiz, go ahead and get divorced. But if you fail it, you have to stay together.*"

That proposition seemed risky to Amelia, but she didn't think his parents would go for it anyway. What adults ever agree to conditions made by kids?

"What are the questions like?" she asked.

"Question number five," he said, reading from the notebook. "What are the two things your son is most afraid of?" He paused.

"And the answer is . . ."

"You really want to know?"

She nodded.

"The first one is obvious," he said. "I'm afraid they actually *will* get divorced."

"But if they really hate each other, maybe it would be better if they *did*," said Amelia.

Casey's answer was simple and immediate: "No." He blinked rapidly. "Now, do you want to know what the second thing is?"

"Sure."

"I'm afraid that something huge and awful will happen on New Year's Eve this year. All over the world." His voice was serious.

"You mean Y2K?"

"Yeah. Aren't you afraid?"

"Not really." She'd heard theories about computers—all kinds—shutting down at midnight on December 31.

"I am. It makes sense—I mean, computers won't know how to deal with the change from nineteen ninety-nine to two thousand. Planes will fall out of the sky. Security systems and elevators will fail. Bank accounts will be frozen."

"I never fly anywhere," said Amelia, thinking of Florida for the first time that day, "and I don't have any money to speak of. *And*—it's only April. They—whoever *they* is—will figure it out by the end of the year." She smiled and threw up her hands nonchalantly, but she could tell by the look on Casey's face that he was deeply concerned.

"Well, I'm worried enough for both of us," he said.

Y2K was the least of her troubles, but Amelia knew that, truthfully, there was nothing she could say to reassure him. And, then, suddenly, she felt alone. So alone. It dawned on her that if there were a quiz about her, no one would know the answers except maybe Mrs. O'Brien and possibly Natalie. She doubted that her father would do very well. No one really knows me, she thought. A hard, glittering realization. It was pathetic, but Dr. Cotton knew her better than anyone.

Then it struck her that *her* greatest fear was that Mrs. O'Brien would die before she, Amelia, left for college. If that happened, what would she do? How could she make it through the string of unbearable days? She shook her head as if to loosen the ugly thought and allow it to fall away. She needed to get her hands into some clay as soon as possible.

11 · A LOT

All morning, while Amelia worked on her clay sculptures, Casey worked on his quiz, except when Louise asked him to clean the sink and take out the garbage. Knowing about the quiz made Amelia feel like she had a secret, and as she rolled the clay between her hands, she also felt infinitely smarter somehow because of it.

From time to time, Casey sat sideways, away from the table, notebook on his lap, and then Amelia wondered if he was seeking a bit of privacy to write a question about her. Might she be mentioned in the quiz? The thought gave her an odd thrill and her face became hot.

Amelia formed five more rabbits that morning. Unlike the rabbits she'd made last week—squatting, alert, with upturned ears—these were lying down with their ears pressed against their bodies. They were smaller than her fist and looked like chalky gray eggs at first glance, or stones.

Amelia was finding her way into a new lump of clay, letting her fingers work out a rhythm before starting another rabbit when Louise tapped her on her shoulder. "Those are lovely," said Louise, looking carefully at the rabbits. "Subtle and beautiful. I didn't know they were rabbits at first. That's what makes them interesting."

"Thank you."

"You should make a lot of them," said Louise. "A lot. If you make enough of them, I'd let you display them in the front window. You could have a little show."

"Really?" Amelia's soul seemed to inflate.

Louise nodded. "I think it could be wonderful. The whole window full of them. A lot of the same thing can look very dramatic. A lot can be very good. You might even glaze them all the same way. Think about it."

There was nothing to think about. *Yes*, she wanted to shout. *Yes, I will make hundreds of rabbits if necessary. Yes, I will display them in the front window.*

Amelia closed her eyes for a full breath. In, out.

Forget not going to Florida. Forget her moody, remote father. Forget the end of the world.

Maybe she could be a real artist. Maybe she had a new friend who shared secrets. Maybe her life really was changing.

12 • FROSTING AND LAMB CHOP

"Frosting," said Amelia. "His name is Frosting."

Casey nodded.

They were at the coffee shop, having a late lunch by the big window, inventing names and stories for people.

Frosting was kicking a stone down the sidewalk. Amelia thought he was six or seven. His tongue was sticking out of the corner of his mouth. His untucked, loose flannel shirt looked like a tent around him. Most distinctive was his hair—it rose up into several rigid white-blond shiny peaks. Hence, his name. The wind picked up and his shirt billowed, but his hair remained stiff, unmoving.

"I like the one-name people," said Amelia.

"Like Feather?"

"Yeah, like Feather. And, now, Frosting."

"Feather would eat him alive," said Casey.

"Yep," Amelia agreed. "She would." She couldn't keep from smiling. She was still glowing from Louise's comments about her rabbit sculptures, and so the story she was concocting for Frosting was joyful. "He's going to find a lottery ticket in the gutter and win ten million dollars, propelling his family out of poverty. And he's super-smart. A genius. He's going to Harvard next fall."

Casey snorted.

Frosting crossed the street and disappeared behind an evergreen hedge.

"This one's mine," said Casey, tipping his head toward a spidery old woman walking uneasily with a slight limp and a thick cane. It seemed as if the wind could lift her up and carry her off. Despite her awkward movements, there was an elegance about her. Her pale moon face was framed by white curls and topped with a brown beret that matched her long coat. Her expression was placid.

The beret brought to mind an acorn. Acorn, Amelia thought. I'd name her Acorn. She tried to send the name to Casey telepathically.

It didn't work.

"Okay," said Casey, adjusting his shoulders, wiggling in his chair, resettling himself. "Here we have—Lamb Chop. She looks like a sweet, respectable old lady, but she's a member of the CIA. The limp is fake. Her cane is a weapon." His voice flickered with merriment. "She's killed several people in active duty. She's brutal."

Amelia laughed. She wanted the way she felt at that very moment to last forever.

But nothing does. In seconds Lamb Chop was gone, and the sidewalk was empty.

13 · EPIPHANY

And then, minutes later, something happened. Something that changed Amelia's world. Shook it up.

Casey had a funny look on his face.

"What?" said Amelia. "What is it?"

"Her," said Casey, pointing. "See that woman?" He lifted an eyebrow, thinned his lips.

Amelia nodded. "What are you naming her?"

"I don't know what I'm naming her . . . but this is weird."

"What's weird?"

"That woman." He was staring at her, hard-eyed.

She looked perfectly ordinary to Amelia. From the side, from this angle, this distance. "What about her?"

"Well . . . you're going to think I'm crazy . . . and I know this is going to sound strange, but I think it's your sign. *She's* your sign." He turned to Amelia to judge her reaction, but she was watching the woman and he couldn't see her expression. His voice became so small. "It's like a movie." Smaller. "She's your mother."

"*What?*" Amelia's heart pinched and she felt a flash of anger. Their innocent naming game had crossed over to a different place. "You really *are* crazy."

"No, listen. I can't explain it exactly. And, yes, it seems impossible, but—it's like one of those *Twilight Zone* episodes from the olden days.

You know, when someone appears from another dimension. It's just this feeling I have. It's eerie."

Casey's cheeks were flushed, his eyes wide, shiny as glass. "I saw the woman earlier, in front of the clay studio. I think I might have seen her yesterday, too. It's like she's hanging around, searching for something—or someone. And look at her—she has red hair like yours and her nose is like yours, too." He took an audible breath. "She looks like you. I mean, she does. Really. A lot."

Did she?

With a bow of his head, Casey kept going. "It's not that she's your mother *exactly*. It's like she's an impression of her. A symbol. Sort of like a ghost, but she's real."

In the stretch of silence that followed, Amelia tucked her hands into her armpits and sharpened her eyes.

This is what she saw. The hair. Undeniably

similar. The familiar nose. Better looking on a middle-aged woman. The serious way the woman walked. (That's how *I* want to walk, thought Amelia.) Her distinct shape against the neighborhood scene, beneath a blue unbroken sky. The jacket. Amelia loved the woman's jacket, open and flapping, corduroy the color of cantaloupe, with scalloped lilac trim on the sleeves and hem. Oh, how she loved the jacket. She'd never seen anything like it.

For just a second Amelia felt a separateness from every other person except the woman. And that second seemed to contain her whole life, everything that mattered. And the unfinished things inside her felt complete.

Amelia found it hard to breathe. The world was shrinking to a pinhole.

Now the woman came closer to the window. She whipped her hair into a high, loose bun, using the window as a mirror.

Now she passed right by them, glancing into the coffee shop, a mere sheet of glass separating them. Amelia didn't speak, but with imploring eyes she asked, *Do you know me? Is it me you're looking for? Do I belong to you?*

Now the woman walked out of Amelia's direct line of sight. Out of the world.

Now there was something new in Casey's voice when he said, "It's really true. We've had a sighting. This is significant. This is the strangest thing that's ever happened to me."

And now Amelia whispered, "To *me*."

Perhaps, this, this, was the start of her life.

Strange things always occur in life, she reasoned. Unbelievable things were as common as common ones if you were open to them, she told herself. If you looked beneath the surface.

Miracles did happen. At least, she believed they did. They *could*. Wasn't it true? There are people whose hearts stop and then beat again.

People who are missing for years and then show up one day out of the blue. There are kids who fall from great heights and barely suffer a scratch. If there were six billion people on the planet, couldn't one uncanny, irrational thing happen to one of them, to her? Couldn't she experience something from another dimension? Couldn't she?

"We still have to name her," said Casey. "*You* should. She's your mother. What's your mother's name, anyway?"

Her mother's name was Sabrina, but she didn't want to say it out loud. "I'll call her Epiphany," said Amelia.

"Epiphany's your mother's name?"

"No. Epiphany is my middle name. My mother wanted to call me Epiphany because I was born on January sixth, the Feast of Epiphany."

"What's that?"

"It's the day the Three Kings supposedly visited Baby Jesus with their gifts. But we're not religious and my father thought it was an odd, trendy name. But, anyway, it's my middle name. So that's what I'm calling the woman."

"Your *mother*. That's cool. And, hey, it's another one-word name like Feather."

Your mother. Was this whole thing Casey's way to pass his time in exile at his aunt's? To make the week more interesting? To take his mind off his parents' problems? Was it just a game to him?

Or was something else happening? Some impossible, wonderful, improbable cosmic convergence? A glimpse into an alternative reality, a parallel universe? Through her flawed understanding of the world, could she make this—her mother—possible?

She knew she wouldn't tell anyone. Especially her father and even Mrs. O'Brien.

She didn't want anyone explaining it, making it untrue, pointing out the absurdity of it.

"Are you ready?" asked Casey.

"Ready? For what?"

Seconds ticked past. "I think we should follow her. Come on. Let's go find Epiphany."

14 • THE WIND

Reluctantly, Amelia set off after Casey—out the door and down the street. They went in the direction Epiphany had gone, in pursuit of the flash of her cantaloupe jacket. It was very windy now, as if something had been stirred up. My mother, Amelia thought. Epiphany. That's what—who—had been stirred up.

The jacket was like a bright flag ahead of them.

A blast of wind rushed Amelia's face and she gulped air. For a giddy, dizzying moment, she imagined she'd breathed in the ghostly essence of her mother. And then she felt she might faint at the thought of it. She'd lost her inner balance.

"Hurry," called Casey.

"Coming." She didn't know if this following business was a good idea.

Casey was walking so fast she had to quicken her pace to keep up with him. Boldly, she grabbed his arm to slow him down, startling herself. And him, too, it seemed. They froze for a second, then moved on. Their arms were linked for several strides before dropping.

Amelia welled up with confusion. She didn't know what she wanted to happen. If they caught up to Epiphany, what would they say to her? What would they do? The whole thing—the strangeness of it—was too much. Her poor brain was twisted up like a pretzel.

They turned the same corner Epiphany had, but she'd disappeared. And then when they reached the next corner, they looked in every direction. Epiphany was nowhere to be seen.

After a moment of complete stillness, Casey said, "Gone."

Amelia nibbled on the inside of her cheek.

"Maybe," said Casey, "she really is a ghost. She *vanished*."

"Maybe she's just a woman," said Amelia. "Some woman who has nothing to do with me."

"No," said Casey. "Absolutely not."

They wandered around the neighborhood, turning their heads, looking here and there, but it seemed to Amelia that the chase was over, which made her glad somehow. Several times Amelia thought she heard someone plaintively say her name. But it wasn't Epiphany calling for her daughter; it was the brakes of a passing truck and a squeaky garage door and the wind playing tricks, messing with her head.

The first time she'd heard her name, she'd

said, "Did you hear that?" Her voice was both shy and urgent.

"What?" Casey was excited by the prospect. "What?"

"I don't know." She shook her head. "I thought I heard someone calling me. I'm wrong. It's nothing."

Casey shrugged. "I didn't hear anything. But keep your ears open."

When she'd heard her name again and then again, she felt a mild sadness pressing down on her shoulders, taking hold, but she said nothing.

In fact, neither one of them said much as they meandered, hands shoved into their pockets. After one particularly long silence, dense with thoughts of Epiphany, Amelia announced, "Oh, hey, that's my house." She tipped her head.

"That one?" said Casey, jutting his chin.

"Yeah. Do you want to come inside? There's a good chance there'll be homemade cookies." She waited, shifting uneasily in and out of a pool of deep shadow. For a second she regretted the invitation, thinking he'd respond by saying something about her mother baking the cookies.

But he didn't. He said, "Sure." And they walked through the back door into the kitchen, drawn by the warm golden light.

15 · LUCKY PENNY

"These cookies are exquisite," said Casey.

"Well, thank you," said Mrs. O'Brien. "I'm glad you like them."

"Oh, I do. Thank *you*."

"And you're very polite," added Mrs. O'Brien.

The two of them seemed encased within a circle of mutual appreciation. Amelia watched them, feeling—feeling what? Feeling that seated before her were the two people currently in her daily life she was most comfortable with. Her heart rose up, and she let out a joyful sound—a short, piercing *eeep*.

"What was *that*?" asked Casey, laughing.

"Just a happy, I-love-this-cookie noise," said Amelia, downplaying her happiness.

"As I said: exquisite." Casey reached for another cookie.

"You two are going to make my head swell," joked Mrs. O'Brien.

"That," said Amelia, "would never happen."

"Exquisite," said Casey again, holding up his cookie, admiring it from every angle before taking a big bite.

If any other boy their age had used the word *exquisite*, it would have sounded phony, but Amelia thought that Casey was as sincere as could be. And, he was so different from any boy she knew at school. Not that she knew any of them well.

Sitting at the kitchen table, Amelia wished this moment would last and last, that this scene would grow and unspool and carry her away.

She saw the kitchen as if she'd never seen it before. A hundred thousand things were going on in her head.

Her life tended toward the narrow, the limited, and today, right now, it was leaning toward something different, something more, toward what she imagined most people had every day.

Casey pulled a penny from his pocket and spun it on the tabletop. "I found this today," he said. "A lucky penny. So, I guess it's my lucky day." He stared at the penny as it wobbled and fell flat. "It would have been more lucky if we would have found, you know . . ." His eyes drifted up to Amelia's.

Amelia's heart pounded. She flashed Casey an expression—both disapproving and searching. She was not ready to talk about Epiphany. "Mrs. O'Brien, do you remember when we would plant pennies?" Amelia asked. A diversion.

"Of course I do."

"We haven't done that in a long time," said Amelia.

"What's that?" asked Casey. "How do you plant pennies? And why?"

"It's fun," said Amelia. "It's when you put a penny someplace where you think someone will find it. Like on a railing or a park bench or a windowsill or a shelf in a grocery store."

Mrs. O'Brien smiled. "You used to love to hide and wait and watch to see what would happen."

"Having little kids find them was the best," said Amelia. "Sometimes they'd get so excited."

"That's funny," said Mrs. O'Brien, "because you were little yourself." She paused. "But you've always seemed old. An old soul, you are."

"Here," said Casey. "Yours to plant." He slid the penny across the table to Amelia.

"Oh!" said Amelia, sharply, rising quickly from her chair with a jerk, nearly falling.

"What?" said Casey.

"You're jumpy," said Mrs. O'Brien calmly. "Poor thing, what is it? What's the matter?"

"I heard a car door," said Amelia. "I'll see if it's the Professor."

A look of understanding passed between Amelia and Mrs. O'Brien.

"Who's the Professor?" asked Casey.

"Mrs. O'Brien will fill you in," said Amelia. As she left the kitchen, Amelia purposely brushed against Mrs. O'Brien. Just to have the contact, the touch. "I'll be right back."

16 · SCENARIO

The driveway was empty. And so was the street directly in front of their house. From the porch, Amelia glanced left and right. She saw two things. She gasped.

One: Her father's car was approaching from down the block, on the left.

Two: A small silver car was parked at the corner, on the right. Standing beside the car on the driver's side was Epiphany. The cantaloupe jacket was like an exotic bird in a bleak landscape. Epiphany seemed to be looking right at Amelia and when she saw the Professor's car pull into the driveway, she hesitated, then quickly slipped back into the silver car and drove away.

Seeing what Amelia saw was like eating ice cream too fast. Her head ached. And then her heart.

It was a moment of breathless suspension.

Her father slammed the car door—a jolt that brought her back. Back to the porch, watching her father move against the wind under the pewter sky, toward her, smiling tightly.

She moved and acted as expected—greeting her father, introducing him to Casey, filling a few awkward minutes with small talk until her father fled to the privacy of his study. But she did so on liquid legs, as if in a fog, her composure paper-thin.

She hoped no one sensed her remove.

Epiphany had taken hold of her imagination. Amelia's thoughts lit up with possible scenarios.

The scenario that blazed brightest was this: Amelia's mother hadn't died. For some reason, long ago, she needed to leave her husband and two-year-old daughter. And, now, after ten years, she'd returned. Because she couldn't bear to live without her daughter.

The details of the story, the explanation, might be surprising, even painful to hear, but it would be worth it. The tearful reunion. The ongoing life. The future.

Amelia, Casey, and Mrs. O'Brien were still in the kitchen. Amelia was working hard to hide her tumultuous feelings. Her stomach rumbled and she said, "I guess I'm getting hungry again," but she wasn't hungry at all.

When Casey excused himself to use the bathroom, Mrs. O'Brien offered a suggestion. "You could ask him to stay for dinner," she said quietly.

But Amelia wanted him to leave. She didn't want to discuss Epiphany, this new development, but she was too preoccupied because of it to act normally. "Thanks, but no," said Amelia. She shrugged. "You know, the Professor might be weird." She shrugged again and shook her head.

"If you change your mind . . ." Mrs. O'Brien's voice trailed off.

When Casey returned to the kitchen, Amelia told him there was something she needed to do and that he should go. She played with her hands as she spoke, pressing her fingertips together, then forming a bowl with her hands in midair.

"Well, see you tomorrow then," said Casey, a touch of disappointment in his voice. "Come to the studio early," he added, hopeful.

"Okay," replied Amelia.

But she knew Casey would understand if she didn't show up because Epiphany had come back for good. In her cantaloupe jacket. In the silver car. The long-lost mother. Home.

17 · TOO BIG

Amelia looked for the silver car from the living room window several times throughout the rest of the day. The car was nowhere to be seen. Although she was ready to burst, Amelia kept the earlier Epiphany sighting to herself, hoarding it, the biggest secret she'd ever held.

When Mrs. O'Brien spotted Amelia at the window, she said, "Honey, I don't think he's coming back. You asked him to leave."

"Oh, I know," said Amelia. "Just checking the weather."

Dinner was a quiet affair, equal parts Mrs. O'Brien's even regularity and the Professor's expressions of irritated disappointment. During the silences, Amelia thought about Epiphany. The scenario she'd been creating deepened. Among the swirl of possibilities were travels to faraway places and important jobs, but no other children. Just one mother and one daughter. Amelia knew Epiphany was the mother and that she, Amelia, was the daughter. She knew it in her bones, her teeth.

If she were more brave, Amelia would have pulled Mrs. O'Brien from the table into the pantry off the kitchen and begged her to answer the questions that filled her head:

What do you think about my mother?

What really happened to her?

Is she alive?

Tell me everything, she wanted to implore. But, of course, she couldn't. And didn't.

But she made it through. Through dinner. And through the long, lonely hours before bed.

At one point, when she heard her father go into the bathroom, Amelia sneaked into his study.

Quickly, she looked at the small photograph of her mother. It was in a gold frame on his desk.

Was it a photo of Epiphany? Amelia didn't know. Her mother was so young in the picture. It could be her, she thought. She heard the toilet flush down the hall and fled.

In bed, in the dark nothingness of her room, she talked to Dr. Cotton; it was like a little play. She imagined his reassuring voice, his firm questions.

Amelia: *I guess I'm afraid.*

Dr. Cotton: *Of what?*

Amelia: *Life.*

Dr. Cotton: *What about it?*

Amelia: *It's too big.*

Dr. Cotton: *How so?*

Amelia (after a long pause): *It's so big that I don't know what will happen.*

The next thing Amelia knew it was morning. Dr. Cotton sat on his shelf, mute and lifeless. Same as always. It seemed nothing in the world had changed. But then she remembered Epiphany and she sensed that the world would never be the same.

18 · NOTHING

According to Mrs. O'Brien's breakfast report, the day promised to be a gentler one, with a delicate blue sky, a warming sun, and only a slight breeze. It was still chilly, she'd said, but Amelia took the weather as a sign—a good sign—that today would be an important day.

Amelia bent the shape of her morning to accommodate Epiphany, forgoing the clay studio and Casey. She wanted to be home in case Epiphany came back. Amelia's waking dream, her fantasy, involved a reunion scene in the front yard that caused her skin to tingle when she considered it.

Amelia waited, but nothing happened. Epiphany didn't ring the doorbell. She didn't telephone. There was no silver car out front. Nothing.

Amelia ended up spending a good part of the morning in the yard. Maybe the silver car would drive by; even a glimpse of it would sustain her. The dingy lawn was littered with twigs and branches from the previous day's wind. Amelia drifted about, hunched over, picking up sticks and piling them by the curb, something she'd seen her father do.

She was marking time. And time had slowed. Drip, drip, drip.

"Looking for spring?" It was Mrs. O'Brien. She came down the porch steps and approached Amelia. She was wearing an oatmeal-colored sweater with big wooden buttons over her pastel shirt. Her arms were folded tightly across her chest.

Amelia started. She'd been staring at a twig, rubbing the little nub at the tip, but her mind had been spinning with a detail from her waking dream. "I realized how much I needed you," Epiphany said in the dream. Amelia had replayed the line several times, drawing out the word *needed* and pumping it full of emotion until she felt purely exulted.

"Oh, hi," said Amelia, turning. She rose and dropped the twig onto the pile. She knew she was blushing.

"Honey, I think I know what you're doing," said Mrs. O'Brien. Her fierce gray eyes were watery from the sharp air. Her smile was a bemused smile.

"You do?"

Mrs. O'Brien nodded.

Amelia balled her hands, then opened them, spreading her fingers like the points of a star. Again. Again. "What am I doing?" she whispered. She thought she was tilting.

Mrs. O'Brien grabbed her hands. "Your fingers are freezing!" she said. She pressed Amelia's hands—first one, then the other—between hers, rubbing them gently. "Listen, it's hard to believe, but I know how you feel." She raised her eyebrows as if inviting Amelia to share her tightly held secret.

Was it possible? Did Mrs. O'Brien know what Amelia was feeling?

"Boys are funny creatures," said Mrs. O'Brien. "And I wouldn't wait around for anyone. You. You're the one. People should be waiting for you."

"Oh," said Amelia.

"And you've got a lifetime ahead of you to worry about those kinds of things."

Mrs. O'Brien's misunderstanding became suddenly clear to Amelia, but she didn't know quite what to do. "Oh," Amelia said again. "Yeah. Well . . ."

"And, just so you know, *he's* thinking about *you*." Mrs. O'Brien nodded. "That's right. Two times since you've been out here the phone rang. Both times, when I answered, whoever it was—him, I'm sure—hung up."

"The phone rang?" Amelia's voice jumped. And so did she, just a little.

"Yes, sweetie. Calm down."

"Did he say *anything*?"

"No, but I knew it was him. I know the way you just know these things."

Amelia was already moving toward the porch, staring ahead, unblinking. The grass, the bushes, the house—the world—suddenly seemed muted. And her understanding that Epiphany had been calling was vivid, oh-so-real. Mrs. O'Brien was half a step behind her.

"Maybe she'll call again," said Amelia. "*He'll. He'll* call again."

The simplicity of what was happening, the

reassurance, the affirmation, was pulling her inside—through the hallway to the telephone in the kitchen.

About five minutes later, the phone rang.

"Hello?" said Amelia, breathlessly.

"Oh, good, it's you. Finally. Hi."

Casey's voice was like a black shape coming at her, wiping out her hope.

Amelia was silent.

"Aren't you coming to the studio?" asked Casey.

Silence.

"Hey, Amelia, are you there?"

"Did you call before?" asked Amelia in a quavery voice.

"Yeah."

"Twice?"

"I guess."

"Why did you hang up?"

"I don't know. I guess I was hoping you'd answer. So, are you coming?"

"I don't know."

And then she hung up.

"It was him, wasn't it?" asked Mrs. O'Brien with outstretched arms.

Amelia nodded. "You're always right," she said, letting her disappointed self melt into Mrs. O'Brien.

"Not always."

"Just about," said Amelia.

19 · HEART

After lunch Amelia rushed off to the studio because she needed to get her hands back into some clay. She thought if she stayed home waiting for Epiphany any longer, she might explode. She also felt badly about the way she'd treated Casey. Without explaining anything, she wanted him to know that everything between them was fine.

"Are you mad at me?" asked Casey the second he saw her. He was sitting in his usual place. A heart-shaped slab of clay lay before him on the worktable. He was carving into it with a sharp tool.

"No."

"You hung up on me."

"I know," said Amelia.

He looked at her with narrowed, searching eyes.

She gave a tiny shrug. "It's hard to explain."

He kept looking at her, looking through her, waiting.

"I'm sorry," she said, and then she changed the subject. "What are you working on?"

Now it was Casey's turn to shrug. "Another dumb idea. A heart for my parents." He extended his hands and waved them, as if presenting it.

The heart had dots pressed into the clay around the edges forming a border. In the middle, it said $C + G$.

"The C and the G are for *Charlie* and *Gwen*," Casey explained. "My parents."

"I remember," said Amelia.

"I didn't want you to think the *C* was for Casey."

"I didn't."

"Because then you would have wondered who the *G* stood for."

"Hmmm," Amelia murmured. She lowered her eyes.

Casey's shirt was lime green with the words *Divorce Sucks* written across it in black blocky capital letters. When Amelia noticed it, she said, "I bet your mom loves that one." She nodded at the shirt.

"When she saw it, she said, 'I *hate* that word.' And so I said, 'Oh, good, I'm glad we agree on that. I hate the word *divorce*, too.' Then she gave me one of those looks only a mother knows how to give. You know." Casey paused. He squeezed his eyes shut and opened them as if to clear away his last comment. "Sorry," he said. "Sorry."

"It's okay."

Casey opened his mouth to speak again, and Amelia sensed that he was on the verge of saying something about Epiphany when there was the sudden noise of Louise banging up the stairs.

Louise entered the workroom. "Oh, good, you're here," she said to Amelia. "I just opened the kiln. Your rabbits are too hot to glaze, but they look great."

Amelia smiled.

"Make more," said Louise.

"I will."

Amelia got some clay and started right away. At first she watched Casey out of the corner of her eye. He poked and scraped and stared at his heart; he sprayed it with water from time to time to keep it moist. But soon she became more and more aware of the rabbits she was forming and less aware of anything else. When it was time to leave she had four new rabbits ready to be fired.

"Will you come tomorrow?" Casey asked.

"Yes," she said. "I promise."

Suddenly they seemed shy with each other.

"We can do lunch," Casey said. "Make up names and stories for people again. Look for Epiphany."

Amelia smiled what she knew was a forced, grimace-like smile. She felt completely out of sorts because of Epiphany, imprisoned by the uncertainty. What's really happening? she wondered. I just want to be normal, she thought. Right now, everything's weird.

"Yes," she said, and as she squeezed past him to leave she noticed that the initials on the heart had been changed. Now they were *C* and *A*.

20 · REAL

Walking home, Amelia felt lonelier than ever. Which was strange, and she knew it. Strange, because Casey had written $C + A$ inside his heart. She wondered if the A was for *Amelia*. Normally this would have surprised and excited her. But today, at this moment, she felt cut loose from the world, as if she were separate from herself, watching life happen to a twelve-year-old motherless girl whose mother may or may not have come back from god-knows-where to reclaim her daughter. How could that possibility not cast its shadow—or spread its blinding light—on every single thing?

Amelia opened her hand and traced $C + A$ on

her palm with her finger. Then she made a tight fist as if to make the connection permanent.

She took the long way, always on the lookout for Epiphany—either on foot, or driving the silver car. As she roamed the streets, weaving through the neighborhood, she thought that when she got home she might write a letter to her friend Natalie. She would tell her everything that was happening—from Casey and the initials carved into the heart to Epiphany and the silver car. It would be a kind of relief to tell. Wouldn't it?

Or would Natalie think the letter was a joke, or worse, that she, Amelia, was a complete idiot and never write or speak to her again?

Maybe she wouldn't write the letter. She wondered if writing about Epiphany would make her seem more real or less so. Casey is real, she thought. Focus on that.

She clenched her fist again and continued down the street into the unknown future.

21 · TREE

Minutes later, the future presented itself.

Amelia saw the cantaloupe jacket first, a smear of bright color on the porch in the gathering dusk. She had just crossed the street and was at the corner of her block, three houses away from her own.

Amelia's heart skipped a beat. She moved slowly, barely. It was hard to breathe. And then her father came out onto the porch.

Without thinking, Amelia stepped behind the nearest tree, a big one, watching secretly. She ran her hand along the rough bark, then gripped it. She closed one eye first, then the other. Blinked. Squinted. She hadn't been imagining things. Epiphany and her father were still there.

The Professor seemed almost frantic, his arms and elbows raised and jutting. He twisted and turned, looking up and down the block. Epiphany lifted her shoulders and let them fall. Then Amelia's father leaned into Epiphany as if he were whispering to her. He placed his arm across Epiphany's back and led her down the porch steps to the silver car. They moved as one unit, covering the distance quickly. Epiphany dashed around the car and got in on the driver's side. Amelia's father slipped in on the passenger side. The doors slammed at nearly the same second, and the silver car drove away.

Amelia stood behind the tree, unmoving, like the tree itself. She let it all sink in for a moment, trying to reconstruct and process what she'd just seen, every gesture. Watching Epiphany and the Professor together added a piece of truth, a whole new layer to the story and made it more plausible. Oddly, the fact that her father hadn't been wearing a jacket or coat was what struck her, what was so unlike him, what she'd remember most clearly of the scene.

She rose up on her toes. Something had just happened. Something out of the ordinary. She knew that. The knowing was like an electric charge that shot through her body and made her tremble. And then, with great urgency, she ran up to the house and went inside looking for Mrs. O'Brien.

22 • THE MYSTERY OF THE SITUATION

"I saw her! I saw her!" said Amelia. "Now I know she's real. I saw them together."

Mrs. O'Brien's smile was kind, as always, but it was stretched too wide, as if it could hide the obvious truth that she was thinking hard about what to say, how to respond properly. That moment of thinking was long and it contained the stillness of the room (the kitchen) and the suspension of time and the mystery of the situation and the keenness of Amelia's attention.

"What do you know?" asked Mrs. O'Brien softly.

"What do you mean?"

"Did your father talk to you?"

"No."

"Oh." Now Mrs. O'Brien's hands got busy. They seemed to be in flight, weightless, unable to stop moving. They smoothed Amelia's hair and squeezed her shoulders and brushed aside something from her shirt and touched her cheek. "Poor thing," she said.

"What's happening?" asked Amelia. "I saw them on the porch. I saw them drive off together." And then she asked the question she'd been circling in her head. "Who was the woman with my dad?"

The expression on Mrs. O'Brien's face changed quickly, as though she were running through every possibility in search of the appropriate one. She looked out the window, and when she turned back her face was clouded, unreadable.

Amelia's confusion and powerlessness weighed her down, but she fastened her eyes onto Mrs. O'Brien's and was determined to keep them locked firmly in place until she got a response.

Mrs. O'Brien looked out the window again, shaping her lips. "I don't know what to say," she announced gently and carefully, tossing the statement out into the world like a beach ball lobbed to a toddler.

Amelia kept her gaze steady.

Mrs. O'Brien inhaled and exhaled, a sigh big enough to rearrange the furniture. "It's not my place," she began, her voice crimped with worry and concern. "This is between you and your father. You and your father and—" She stopped herself and looked away once more.

"*And*?" said Amelia. "And *who*? My *mother*?"

"Your *mother*?" Now Mrs. O'Brien looked utterly confused, her deeply lined face a portrait of bewilderment.

There was silence.

Finally Mrs. O'Brien said, "I might be over-stepping. . . ." She licked a finger and rubbed at something on Amelia's cheek. "Hannah Barnes may be a lovely woman, but she is not your mother."

Hannah Barnes? Who, Amelia wondered, is Hannah Barnes?

Mrs. O'Brien studied Amelia. "Honey," she said, "I have no idea what is going on in your head; I haven't the slightest notion what it is you're thinking. But you must talk to your father as soon as he gets back." She paused. "And I haven't a clue where he went."

All at once Amelia felt a rush of longing, a deep hollow ache. Fighting tears, she said, as if she were thinking aloud, "So, she's not my mother." And she let herself fall into Mrs. O'Brien's embrace.

An awareness was dawning that her fantasy

was not going to happen no matter how much she wanted it to, and for a brief, piercing moment she understood, in a new way, that the most important things in her father's world did not always, if ever, include her.

23 • SIDESTEPPING

"I don't understand something," said Mrs. O'Brien.

"I don't understand *anything*," said Amelia.

"Then let's sit down and figure this out," said Mrs. O'Brien. "As best we can," she added. "Seeing as it really should be your father doing this."

As soon as they sat at the kitchen table, the phone rang.

"You get it," said Amelia. "Please." She didn't think she could talk to anyone.

Mrs. O'Brien rose, grabbed the receiver of the old-fashioned wall phone with the long, twisty cord, said hello, and then slipped into the pantry and closed the door.

Amelia sensed that it was her father. She could hear Mrs. O'Brien's muffled voice—rising, rising, then dropping—but she couldn't understand a single word. When Mrs. O'Brien finally emerged from the pantry, her shoulders were squared and her lips were compressed.

"It was him, wasn't it?" asked Amelia.

"If you mean your father, yes."

"What did he say?"

"He said to eat without him. He said he'd be home later. He said he'd talk to you then."

"Is that all?" Amelia asked timidly.

Apparently Mrs. O'Brien didn't hear Amelia. Or was she avoiding the question? She looked at Amelia with gentleness and patience. Then she crossed the kitchen to the stove in quick, neat steps. "This sauce is ready," she said cheerfully. "Let's make pasta and a salad. We'll have a nice dinner."

"Okay," said Amelia. It was good to have something to focus on, because thinking about talking to her father later made her slightly dizzy.

In fact, her thoughts and feelings were dizzy, contrary, running wildly in all directions. She could feel anger at her father rise up inside her, but then she felt pity for him, too. Pity for a man who, when she saw him on the porch in her mind's eye, seemed old and confused and who was without his jacket.

But her self-pity grew stronger. Strongest. She hated feeling sorry for herself, but she couldn't help it. Why do we get the life we're given? she wondered.

At Mrs. O'Brien's request, Amelia stirred the pot of sauce with a wooden spoon. Would she and Mrs. O'Brien figure things out? It seemed that after the phone call Mrs. O'Brien was withdrawing a bit, sidestepping the issues.

Except for the cooking sounds—stirring, chopping, running water—the kitchen was quiet. From time to time Mrs. O'Brien hummed— little, broken pieces of melody—which Amelia found disheartening, since Mrs. O'Brien always seemed to hum when she was worried about something.

"Well, now . . . Oh well, then . . ." Amelia said with a casual hollowness, trying to sound mature. Her comment filled the silence for a few seconds, but it did nothing to fill the hollowness inside her.

21 · WHITE HORSE

The Professor didn't come home.

And he didn't call.

And he didn't come home.

And he didn't call.

Dinner was over. The dishes were done. The kitchen was clean.

For the most part, the dinner conversation had centered on the clay studio. Amelia had told Mrs. O'Brien about Louise's idea for a show. She shared a little more information about Casey, and she asked Mrs. O'Brien if she was worried about Y2K. (She wasn't.) But the elephant in the room had remained the elephant in the room. There was no mention of the Professor, no mention of Hannah Barnes. There was no figuring anything out.

Then a shift occurred. "I'm not waiting any longer," said Mrs. O'Brien suddenly. She drew in a sharp, ragged breath. Her pitch changed. "When your father called, he told me to tell you whatever I thought you needed to know. He said that he thought I'd be better at telling you about . . . about what was going on than he would."

"He did?"

"He did." Mrs. O'Brien's cheeks and forehead were glowing, bright pink. The corners of her mouth turned down, as if she were judging the Professor.

"So, in a nutshell, your father—" Mrs. O'Brien stopped for a beat. "Your father was interested in a woman in his department at the university. Another English professor. From what I understand, they went out for a while, and then your father wanted to break it off because he was worried about how you might feel about the situation."

"How could I feel anything about something I didn't know anything about?"

Mrs. O'Brien nodded. "Good question."

"Did you meet her? Is she nice?"

"I did meet her. They came here for lunch one day when you were at school. And, yes, she seems nice. But I can't say that I know much about her."

Mrs. O'Brien continued, "From what I understand . . . she, Hannah Barnes, didn't—doesn't—want the relationship to end."

Amelia could tell by the hesitation and pauses that Mrs. O'Brien was thinking carefully about each piece of information, each word, and was, most likely, holding back certain things, speaking as vaguely as possible.

"He broke it off, he says, for your sake. He . . . he thought it would be . . . too much for you to deal with. Or at least he's trying to. Break it off."

For Amelia, the world had stopped. It was strange to think of her father in this new way. He'd never had a girlfriend before. At least not that she knew of. None that she'd met. She fixed her gaze on the painting next to the refrigerator. It was a painting of a white horse standing in tall grass. She stared at the white horse. She stared without seeing.

Amelia blinked. "Do you think she looks like my mother?" she asked.

Long pause. The seconds seemed separate, widely spaced, strung out like beads on a cord.

"Yes. Yes, I think she does."

"Do you think she looks like *me*?"

Another pause. "Yes. You know, it's not uncommon for people to . . . find people who look like . . . the person who . . . oh, you know what I mean, honey."

Amelia yawned. It was getting late. "Do you think he got in an accident?"

"No."

"Do you think he and his girlfriend took off on a trip?"

Mrs. O'Brien laughed. "Given how much your father loves to travel—no."

Mrs. O'Brien rose from the table. She walked over to Amelia and gave her an awkward hug from behind. "I don't know where he is," she said. "I don't know why he hasn't come home yet."

Because he's a coward, thought Amelia.

"Why don't you sleep over at my house tonight?" said Mrs. O'Brien. "It'll be just like old times, when you were little. I'll write him a note."

There was an understanding between

them that was bigger than words. Deeper. Ultimately, Mrs. O'Brien knew what to say and when to say it. She knew what to do and how to get it done.

Amelia's throat had begun to close. She turned toward Mrs. O'Brien. She smiled through tight lips and she nodded.

25 · SLEEPOVER

Mrs. O'Brien's house was familiar and strange at the same time. It was right across the street, and yet it seemed a world away, a house in a foreign land. Amelia had slept over at Mrs. O'Brien's several times when she was little, but she hadn't in years. In fact, she hadn't set foot in the house in quite a while. But the smell when she entered it met her like an invisible curtain and she felt a jolt of recognition.

Like Mrs. O'Brien, the house smelled clean and soapy—not too perfumy, not too citrusy, not spicy. If clear water had a smell, thought Amelia, this would be it. Amelia drew in a deep breath and exhaled slowly as she followed Mrs. O'Brien down the narrow hallway lined with old photographs to the guest room.

The room was painted periwinkle blue and was decorated with four framed paintings Amelia had done when she was probably four or five. A cat formed of circles and triangles. A purple and pink rainbow. A sun above a row of flowers that looked like little suns. A butterfly. The big bed that took up most of the room was covered with a patchwork quilt.

"Here's an extra blanket," said Mrs. O'Brien. "Just in case."

"Thank you," said Amelia. She took the blanket and placed it at the foot of the bed. She already had her pajamas on. Dr. Cotton was tucked into her backpack in case she needed him.

Mrs. O'Brien stood in the open doorway. She leaned back into the room. "I left him a note. Just get a good night's sleep. Tomorrow's another day."

"Good night," said Amelia.

"Good night." Mrs. O'Brien didn't leave. Her fingers fluttered up and down the doorframe. "I still don't understand something," she said. "Why, earlier, did you say 'So, she's not my mother'? How could she be your mother? I feel like I'm missing something."

Amelia shrugged. She did not want to explain her fantasy about Epiphany. "It was nothing, really. I was just thinking out loud. Weird. I'm weird."

"Life is a sweet, sad mystery," said Mrs. O'Brien, moving toward the bed. "And you are the least weird person I know." She kissed the top of Amelia's head and was gone.

Alone (with Dr. Cotton), under the patchwork quilt, in the moonless dark, the sweet, sad mystery of life seemed impossible to comprehend.

Once, a long time ago, Mrs. O'Brien had told Amelia about her husband. How he had died of cancer when they were newly married. How she'd always wanted children, but never had any. How her husband's death had bonded her with Amelia's father.

Amelia had been too young to mourn her mother's death. She hadn't experienced the death of a loved one the way her father and Mrs. O'Brien had.

But maybe she was now. In a way. Losing Epiphany felt like a death, as if Amelia's mother were dying again. There'd been an opening in Amelia's life and her mother's spirit had entered, come back for a second chance. And, now, the opening had closed.

Amelia sank into the bed. She tried to get comfortable, to let go, to get to the fuzzy edge of sleep. The mattress, like a giant marsh-mallow, rose up around her, swallowed her.

Suddenly, despite everything, she felt more tired than ever.

Sleep, at home, would have been difficult. But sleep at Mrs. O'Brien's, in the big bed, was possible. Like sailing off in a soft, safe boat— on to tomorrow, to morning, to the inevitable talk with her father.

26 · A BARRAGE OF QUESTIONS

Amelia woke early, emerging from a dream that was nearly beyond her grasp. All she could remember was that Epiphany was in it. "Hannah Barnes," Amelia whispered. "Her name is Hannah Barnes."

As the dream slipped away, a question materialized out of the morning air. It came unbidden as Amelia stretched under the covers, and was still nagging at her when she went home.

The question: *Was Hannah Barnes following me?*

And then another question: *Why?*

When Amelia came out of her bedroom after

putting her backpack and Dr. Cotton away, her father was in the hallway, waiting.

"Good morning," said her father.

"Hi."

"Is this a good time for you?"

Amelia nodded.

"Let's go down to the kitchen," said her father.

Amelia followed him.

"How was it? Sleeping at Mrs. O'Brien's?" he asked over his shoulder.

"It was good. Fine."

Going down the stairs, Amelia was right behind her father. She tried to match his footsteps, making a game out of it. If we're in perfect rhythm, she thought, we'll have an okay talk. If not . . .

When they entered the kitchen, Mrs. O'Brien, who'd been rinsing something in the sink, left without a word.

"Did you eat?" her father asked.

Amelia nodded.

"Well," her father began. He stood behind one of the chairs, grasping it tightly. Amelia imagined him standing behind her, squeezing her shoulders. "Well," he said again.

Amelia looked at her hands and said nothing, waiting for him to continue.

The house seemed especially quiet. The morning sun made a pool of light on the table between them and coins of light on the wall.

After clearing his throat, her father said, "I think Mrs. O'Brien explained the situation. Am I right?"

"Well, sort of."

"Do you have any questions?"

Of course, she had questions. But she wanted him to be the parent, to explain things himself, to make things so clear that, perhaps, she wouldn't have questions. "This is our talk?" she wanted to say. But she didn't.

She looked at him and looked away. Looked at him and looked away. He reminded her of a self-portrait of Vincent van Gogh she'd seen in Chicago on a school trip. A trim beard. An orange mustache like a giant frown. Piercing eyes. A high forehead and a prominent brow. A certain gruffness.

"Why didn't you tell me about her?" she asked. "You never tell me anything."

"I didn't think there was anything to tell."

"But there was. Is."

"It's not easy for me to talk about certain things," he told her, looking remote as an unknown star. "You know that." His discomfort showed in his eyes and in the way his shoulders drooped. There were more, frequent throat clearings, and then he said, "I'm sorry," with a gentleness that seemed clumsy, even cautious.

The apology made a crack and she wanted

to slip in a question before her sudden urge to be brave—a flicker—disappeared.

"I do have a question," she said.

"All right."

"Is it possible that the woman on the porch—"

"Hannah," said her father.

"Hannah," Amelia repeated. "Is it possible that Hannah—" She wanted to say *was following me?*, but she couldn't get the words out. Already the flicker had passed; her bravery had vanished.

She held back, changed course. Maybe it was better to keep this to herself. Her father wasn't good at this kind of thing—talking openly—and, therefore, neither was she. So, she said, "Um, is she nice? Do you like her? Can I meet her?"

"That's a *barrage* of questions," he replied. He laughed. And after he laughed there was a change. You could almost see him thinking, the wheels turning. His grip on the chair loosened and so did his face. He blinked a few times, then winked at her. "Yes, yes, and yes," he said. "Now, remember," he added, "I don't know if there's a future with this relationship. Frankly, I'm not quite sure where we stand at the moment." He paused. "I don't want to upset you."

"Maybe I'll like her. You can't say something will upset me if I don't know anything about it." The bravery had returned. Just a little. "You can't use me as an excuse," she told him.

"Life is opera, isn't it? If you look at it a particular way, in a certain light." He sounded like a book, as he often did. "Well, then," he said, backing out of the room. "Here we are. I guess that's that."

Nothing was resolved. There was a vagueness to their discussion, and yet, Amelia felt relieved. There'd been a heaviness in her chest and it was gone for now.

Here we are, she thought. Here we are.

Where exactly?

She wasn't sure.

27 · SWEEPING

"What happened?" asked Amelia.

"There's been a little accident," said Louise.

The floor of the studio was littered with pieces of clay.

"Is that Casey's Eiffel Tower?" asked Amelia.

"*Was*," said Louise. "Yes."

"What happened?" Amelia asked again.

"Careful," said Louise, avoiding the question. "Watch your step." She was sweeping the pieces into a pile.

"Can I help?" asked Amelia.

"Sure. Grab the dustpan."

They worked together—Louise sweeping from one side of the room to the other, Amelia holding the dustpan and then dumping the clay pieces into the garbage can.

Among the fragments of the Eiffel Tower, Amelia saw pieces of Casey's heart. She guessed that neither of them—the tower nor the heart—had been dropped. They looked as if they'd been deliberately smashed, broken to bits.

"Where's Casey?" asked Amelia. She held her breath.

Louise stared at the broom, looking thoughtful for a second. "He said he was going to walk around the block. He should be back any minute. He needed to cool off."

"Is he okay?"

"I hope so."

They worked silently. After a few minutes, Louise leaned the broom against the wall. "I'm going to see if I can find him. I'll be right back."

Amelia grabbed the broom and finished sweeping the floor. She noticed a piece of clay in the far corner that was bigger than most of the others. It was from Casey's heart, and it had her initial carved into it—a slightly crooked capital *A*. She picked it up and shoved it into her pocket.

She was still processing her talk with her father, and now she had this to think about. She'd come to the clay studio eager to make more rabbits and to tell Casey about Epiphany aka Hannah Barnes.

She'd wondered what Casey would think about the new information, what he would say. Now she wondered what had happened to the Eiffel Tower and to his heart and to him.

Life, she thought, just keeps coming at you, one big shapeless surprise after the other. Again. Again.

When, minutes later, Louise and Casey

came through the front door, Amelia could tell that Casey had been crying. His eyes were red and his cheeks looked raw as if they'd been scratched or scribbled on with a crayon.

"Thank you for cleaning up, Amelia," said Louise. "I'm going down to check the kiln." She gave Casey a long look and patted his shoulder. "You know where I am if you need me," she said as she left.

After a little silence, for the third time that morning, Amelia asked, "What happened?"

"My parents are marriage retreat dropouts," said Casey. "Failures. They're on their way home. They're picking me up today. 'We need to talk,' my mom said. 'We need to work out a plan.'" He shrugged and turned away, looking out the window for several seconds. "They're going to get divorced."

"That's awful," said Amelia. "I'm sorry." Now she understood why the Eiffel Tower had been in pieces on the floor. She inched closer to Casey. He was blinking. Blinking back tears, she thought.

"When I found out, I smashed the Eiffel Tower and the heart," he said. He shrugged and blinked again. "I wanted to smash everything," he added, his voice squeaky.

Amelia didn't know what to say.

"At least you still have Epiphany," said Casey.

"Well, no, I don't," said Amelia. "More bad news."

"What?"

"As it turns out, Epiphany is not my mother," Amelia began tentatively.

Casey tilted his head and seemed to shrink. He looked as if he might collapse under some invisible weight, under the strain of more disappointment. He almost looked angry. "How do you know?"

"She came to my house. I saw her on my porch. She was talking to my dad."

"What?"

"She's my dad's girlfriend. Sort of. Who, apparently, looks like my mother. I haven't yet, but I guess I'm going to meet her."

Casey's mouth made a circle, then thinned to a line. "But why was she by the clay studio and the coffee shop, like she was looking for you?"

"I don't know." Amelia shrugged. "I have to figure that out."

"Will you call her Epiphany?"

"No. Her name's Hannah. Hannah Barnes."

"I like Epiphany better," said Casey. He spotted a shard under a chair. He picked it up and threw it away. "I think my aunt is going to be finding those for months." He nudged the garbage can with his foot and gave it a little kick. "Hey, maybe you'll call her Mom."

"I don't think so," said Amelia. She had the sudden urge to shout: *I will never have a mother—she's dead—and, to top it all off, my father never tells me anything.* "Not likely," she said. "No."

Casey sniffed and wiped his nose with the back of his hand. Then he looked right at Amelia and said, "You're lucky. Life is so unfair. I have divorce in my future, and you have a *wedding* in yours."

The comment startled Amelia into silence.

They were both entering uncharted territory as far as parents were concerned. Her mind raced forward, a crazy rush of improbable, pointless possibilities, but there was nothing she could think of to say.

28 · GONE

How do you say goodbye?

Amelia didn't think she'd done it well.

Casey's parents showed up at the studio and Amelia got a glimpse of his life—a life that had nothing to do with her. As his parents slipped back into his world, Amelia slipped out of it. It wasn't a pleasant reunion. Casey rejected hugs from both his parents, standing rigid with an expressionless face. A face as blank as could be. Feeling like an intruder, Amelia whispered goodbye and awkwardly edged away with a gentle wave.

And just like that, Casey was gone, or

rather, she was gone. And the sadness Amelia was left with was profound, because she had a feeling she might never see him again.

Throughout the afternoon, Amelia had the sensation that Casey had fallen through a trapdoor, and after dinner, when her father went to his study, she asked Mrs. O'Brien if she'd stay longer than usual to play cards because she wanted to be with someone. She didn't want to be alone to wallow in her sadness. The stillness of the house at night made the sadness worse.

The kitchen was full of shadows, but at the table beneath the overhead lamp, Amelia and Mrs. O'Brien were enclosed by a circle of yellow light. The moon out the window was like a curl of neon—a bright flourish in the solemn darkness.

They played double solitaire. Between games, as they shuffled their cards, Mrs. O'Brien said, in a hushed voice, "You poor thing. From

142

what you've told me, today was quite a day."

Amelia nodded. "It was."

"Maybe the boy—Casey—will come back soon."

"Or maybe I'll never see him again. The look on his face . . . He was so upset. . . ." Amelia wondered where Casey was at this very moment. Was he with both his parents? She wondered how the rest of the week would be without him. Lonely. That's how it would be.

Mrs. O'Brien started setting up her cards for another game. "I have a feeling you'll hear from him," she said. "And, you always have Louise to keep you up-to-date."

"I guess," said Amelia.

The only sound was the rhythmic, soothing *snap-snap-snap* of the cards until Mrs. O'Brien asked, "What are you thinking about Hannah Barnes?"

The question surprised Amelia. She gripped

143

her cards so tightly her hand hurt. She imagined the ghost of her mother whispering a proper answer in her ear. But her mother, Epiphany, and Hannah Barnes had become a confusing, complicated combination, a wispy presence she might never pin down clearly again. "Actually, I'm thinking that I'd like to meet her."

"Your father said that was possible, right?"

"He did, but you know him. If I don't remind him a million times, nothing will happen."

"Do you want me to say something to him?"

Amelia's fingers flickered across the tabletop as if she were working some magic over her cards, over her life. "Would you?"

"Of course," Mrs. O'Brien said firmly. "I'll be your go-between. Maybe dinner would be nice. Not at a restaurant. Here. I could cook."

"Yes," said Amelia. "Then you'd be around if I needed you." I'll always need you, she thought.

Mrs. O'Brien tapped her cards on the table. Amelia couldn't tell what she was thinking. Her face gave nothing away.

"Are you ready?" asked Mrs. O'Brien lightly, lifting the burden of the day. "Let's play."

29 · A LETTER AND A CAKE

That night Amelia fell asleep quickly, as if under a spell. And she slept deeply. And she slept late. When she woke it was almost noon.

Louise called to say that Casey was back at his house and fine and that Amelia should come to the clay studio.

But Amelia stayed home. She stayed near Mrs. O'Brien all day. They cleaned the living room windows. They reorganized the refrigerator. They baked a chocolate cake with buttercream frosting for no special occasion. "Just because," said Mrs. O'Brien. "Just because."

When the mail arrived, there was a letter

from France, from Natalie. It came exactly when Amelia needed it most.

Dear Amelia,

   I miss you!

   I'm sorry I haven't written in such a long time. We were in Paris last week, which was fabulous, except the place we stayed was so small that Hope and I had to share a room the size of a shoebox. She's driving me crazy. Were we so annoying when we were six? Sometimes I think you're lucky being an only child. I got you a beautiful silver dish at a flea market. It's shaped like a clamshell. I'll bring it when we come home. Did I say I miss you?

   Love,

   Natalie

P.S. The real reason I wrote this letter (which I never mentioned in the letter) was to say that I hope we're still best friends.

Amelia read the letter so many times she practically knew it by heart. She couldn't believe that Natalie had been thinking the same thing she'd been thinking, that she'd doubted their friendship.

Amelia wanted to write Natalie the perfect letter in return. Most important, she'd confirm their friendship. But she would also tell her about Casey and Hannah Barnes. She realized how much her life had changed since Natalie's family had gone to France.

Amelia went to her room to get paper and an envelope. When she reappeared in the kitchen, Mrs. O'Brien said, "Well, as my grandmother used to say, 'Be careful what you wish for.'"

"What?" asked Amelia.

Mrs. O'Brien tugged at her shirt, then smoothed it. She fingered the pearls around her neck. "Hannah Barnes is coming for dinner tonight."

"She is?"

"She is."

"How do you know?"

"Your father just called. I'd asked him about it this morning before he left for his office. I didn't expect him to respond this quickly."

"Tonight?"

"Tonight," said Mrs. O'Brien. "I'm glad we made our cake."

"Should we decorate it?" asked Amelia.

"Yes," said Mrs. O'Brien. "Good idea."

They mixed green and yellow frosting, and Mrs. O'Brien helped Amelia pipe delicate yellow flowers and buds atop curly green stems. The cake had looked perfectly nice and unfussy before, but now it was beautiful. It had been transformed.

Amelia was adding a finishing touch—a pattern of yellow dots around the sides. "What do you think I should wear?"

"Whatever you want," said Mrs. O'Brien. "What you have on is fine."

Of course that's what Mrs. O'Brien would say. But Amelia wanted to be transformed, like the cake. As she placed each dot she asked a question in her head. It became a chant: *What should I wear? How should I act? What should I say? Who should I be?*

Dot. Dot. Dot. Dot. Dot.

"Sweetie," said Mrs. O'Brien gently. "If you think any louder, I'll need earplugs. Don't worry. Just be yourself."

30 · WHAT WAS ACTUALLY HAPPENING

In the front hallway, when they were officially introduced, and Hannah Barnes extended her hand and said, "I've been waiting to meet you," Amelia felt a shiver run down her spine. For a moment, as their fingers made contact, Amelia's fantasy became real once again. The words *Epiphany* and *Mother* flitted across her mind and nearly touched her lips. And then, just as quickly, Amelia was back in the present, and what was actually happening was more than enough to put her in a heightened state.

Although she was certain that Mrs. O'Brien

had cooked a delicious meal, Amelia ate but didn't really taste anything. She was too busy watching Hannah Barnes. Dinner began as one could expect, with stiffness and shyness and uncertainty and politeness setting the mood. Amelia was quiet as a clenched fist. But gradually the mood shifted. Hannah Barnes was easy, bright, warm—a catalyst for conversation. She smiled a lot and looked right at Amelia when she asked a question or listened to the answer. Her eyes were speckled—green and gold—like marbles.

After the slow start, dinner unfolded so pleasantly that Amelia wondered if it could be true. Mrs. O'Brien was her proficient, ideal self. But her father was more talkative than usual, and funny. A minor miracle of everyday life, taking place in an ordinary dining room.

"That was wonderful," said Hannah. "You're a wonderful cook, Mary."

It was jarring to Amelia when anyone called Mrs. O'Brien Mary. Even her father called her Mrs. O'Brien.

"Thank you," said Mrs. O'Brien. "But wait until you see dessert." She glanced at Amelia. "Our cake is something to behold."

Amelia and Mrs. O'Brien cleared the table. In the kitchen, the swinging door closed behind them, Mrs. O'Brien whispered, "What do you think? She's nice, isn't she?"

Amelia bit her lip and nodded. "She is. She really is."

"I'll take the plates and a knife," said Mrs. O'Brien. "You carry the cake."

Amelia didn't want to like Hannah Barnes too much. She needed to protect herself. "What do you think will happen? With her? And Dad?"

"Well, you know your father," said Mrs. O'Brien. "I think—" She stopped. "I think this cake is beautiful," she said in a much louder voice. Cheerful. She held the door open for Amelia.

Proudly, Amelia walked back into the dining room, carrying what she had to admit was a work of art.

31 · NONSENSE AND SORROW

Everyone loved the cake.

Everyone said so.

Everyone had seconds.

"It really is beautiful, you two. Look at this," said Hannah, pointing with her fork to a yellow flower on her piece of cake.

"That was Amelia's doing," said Mrs. O'Brien. "She knew exactly where to place the flowers. She has the touch, a true knack."

"She's an artist," said her father. "She's a real artist." He smiled a little, looking pleased.

Amelia felt a swooshing in her stomach. It was a good feeling. She'd never heard him say this before. Who cared that he was talking about flowers made of frosting?

"Your animals are lovely, too," said Hannah. She tipped her head, indicating the grouping of Amelia's sculptures on the sideboard. "Your dad says you've been working with clay for a long time."

"Since she was a baby," said Mrs. O'Brien.

"Do you like to draw or paint?" asked Hannah.

"Drawing is okay," said Amelia. "Painting, too. But doing ceramics is what I like best."

"Well, you're very good at it," said Hannah.

It was almost too much to take in. Too good to be true. This dinner was not a flight of Amelia's imagination; it was real life.

Carried away by her happiness, like a twig in a stream, Amelia told them about the possibility of a show at the clay studio.

"I'd have the whole front window," said

Amelia, her voice brimming with excitement. "Just me." She told them about making her rabbits—a lot of them. "I already made a bunch. I'll glaze them all the same way. I'm trying to make them all look identical," she told them, talking faster. "Louise said that a *lot* of something is beautiful." She sat back and took a breath.

"I disagree," said her father.

"What?" said Amelia, confused.

"I disagree," he repeated. "Just because there's a *lot* of something doesn't make it beautiful."

Everyone was silent for a few long seconds.

Amelia frowned.

"A lot of *nonsense*?" her father said. "A lot of *sorrow*? That doesn't sound so beautiful to me."

Amelia's heartbeat quickened. Her happiness was thinning to threads. She didn't know what to do or say. But she felt a snarl of fury inside her and she thought she might cry. Abruptly, she pushed herself away from the table. "Two things you know a lot about," said Amelia as she fled. "Nonsense and sorrow."

"Amelia, come back," her father called. "I didn't mean to upset you. I'm sorry."

She went to her room and closed the door. "Thanks, *Dad*," she said to no one. "Thanks for ruining my life."

32 · JUST RIGHT

While Amelia lay on her bed crying quietly, she heard voices in the hallway. She heard her father. She heard Mrs. O'Brien. She heard Hannah.

She sat up and listened. She couldn't make out what they were saying. Just snatches of voice, no words. Her father's voice was the first to go away. Then, after a minute, Mrs. O'Brien's and Hannah's voices were gone, too.

Silence. But a presence lingered.

Then a soft knocking on the door.

"Come in," said Amelia, her voice weak and scratchy.

She expected Mrs. O'Brien and was surprised and embarrassed when Hannah slowly entered her room. She hid her face.

"May I?" asked Hannah, pointing to the bed.

Amelia nodded. Her eyes shone with tears.

Hannah sat beside Amelia. Neither spoke for a long time, then Hannah said, "Are you okay?"

Amelia nodded again.

"I had to talk them into letting me come in here. Your father and Mrs. O'Brien were afraid you wouldn't want me. But I wanted to." Hannah inched closer to Amelia. "He really loves you, you know," she said. "And you know this better than I do—he has a hard time showing how he feels and dealing with things head-on."

Hannah's arm touched Amelia's shoulder. The soft pressure was a surprising comfort.

"There's something you should know," said Hannah. "He was worried, so worried, that you'd be upset if he and I were together. And when he couldn't tell you—wouldn't ask you if it was okay with you—I wanted to ask you myself. Because I wanted this to work out. So the other day, on impulse, I walked by the clay studio. Then I did it again. I hoped I'd just run into you by chance in the neighborhood."

Hannah moved her fingers as if she were playing a piano on her lap. She smiled and raised her eyebrows. "I never found you," she said. She stilled her hands and laced her fingers together. "Well, that's not exactly true. I have to confess something. I think I *did* see you at that little coffee shop on Regent Street, but I chickened out. I didn't want to embarrass you. And, I realized I had no idea what to say to you. I was afraid, I guess."

"Really?"

"Yes. Crazy, huh? Adults are afraid, too."

Amelia tried to swallow a gasp. "Oh," she managed to say. Things were clicking into place in her mind, making sense.

"I felt like a stalker," said Hannah. "It was not my best idea." Strands of her hair were falling from her loose bun. Coppery tendrils framed her face. She played with one of them, twirling it. "He'd shown me a photo of you once. I kept thinking I saw you. Everywhere I went. But I liked him enough to do it. To look for you, to try to talk to you." She flicked her hair away from her eyes, tucked a stray piece behind her ear. "I realized it wasn't the right way to go about it—and I couldn't do it, talk to you, without your father."

Amelia regarded her seriously, listening to every word as if her very life depended on it.

Hannah turned, looking directly at Amelia. "All of this is to say that tonight was very difficult for him. He wanted everything to be perfect. For you to like me. For me to like you. And I know he didn't mean what he said about your show. He's so proud of you."

There didn't seem to be a proper response. Amelia leaned into Hannah, seemed to collapse against her, and as she did, she collapsed inside. She started to cry again and she wouldn't have been able to say why, exactly. She cried for everything, everyone—her mother, her father, Mrs. O'Brien, Epiphany, Hannah, Casey. Herself.

Pulling away just a bit, Hannah said, "You know, when you were little, he walked you to sleep every night. He couldn't put you in your crib if you were still awake—you'd just cry. He told me that he'd give you a postcard. You loved it apparently. It was of Babar, the elephant. So you'd clutch your beloved postcard and he'd hold you over his shoulder and carry

163

you all around the house, bouncing you and swaying. He knew you'd fallen asleep when you dropped the postcard. Then he could put you in your crib."

"I wonder where my mom was?"

"I think she was already sick."

"He never told me about this."

"That's just the way he is, I guess."

"But he told *you*."

"Only because I found the postcard stuck behind a pile of books and file folders in his office at school. And it didn't seem like the kind of thing he'd keep around. So, I asked him about it."

Side by side, something passed between them. By now, Hannah's bun was completely undone. She quickly and smoothly raked up her hair and twisted and pulled it back into place.

"Will you do that for me?" asked Amelia.

Without saying a word, Hannah reached into her pocket. She held up an elastic band with a small blue bead for Amelia to see. Then she repositioned herself on the bed. Gently, she gathered Amelia's hair and worked it into a bun. Not too tight, not too loose. Just right.

33 · HUMAN FRAILTY

"Why don't you show me what you're working on," her father said the next morning.

Amelia looked at him curiously.

"At the clay studio," he added.

They were in the kitchen; breakfast was done. Mrs. O'Brien brushed past Amelia's father and gave his arm a squeeze. "That's nice," she said.

Amelia could hardly believe this was happening, but then, lately, her life had been full of surprising things. "Yeah, sure," she said. "Okay."

Her father hadn't said anything directly about last night. He hadn't talked about

Hannah or about how the night had ended. This wasn't normal fatherly behavior, she guessed, but it wasn't atypical for him. But he was gentle with her at breakfast. And she understood his asking to go to the clay studio as his way of trying to make it up to her.

On the walk to the studio, Amelia was in a thoughtful mood. The sun was shining, then cut off by clouds, then shining again. Something about the mild air and the quality of light as it came in shafts through the branches convinced her that spring was finally a possibility.

"Well, that's a sure sign of spring," said her father, suddenly. Someone—obviously a child—had drawn with chalk on the sidewalk in front of them. There were crude tulips with pointy petals and scribbly bumblebees as big as basketballs and the crooked outline of a hopscotch game with some of the numbers written backward.

Amelia made her way through the squares, hopping on one foot. She felt silly, but only slightly. It was fun and it reminded her of being little.

"Look," said Amelia. "No kid did *that*." In big, blue loopy cursive writing, the sentence *How is human frailty connected to love?* covered two whole squares of the sidewalk.

"Must be a philosopher," said Amelia's father.

"Or an English professor," said Amelia.

He laughed deeply and picked up his pace.

At the clay studio, Amelia turned shy. She liked that Louise left them alone after saying hello and giving a quick Casey update.

Amelia led her father to the shelf that held the rabbits she'd been working on, as well as some other pieces from weeks past. She explained how some pieces were still drying; some were fired, ready to be glazed; some were glazed, ready to be fired again.

He examined them closely, moving slowly along the shelf, running his fingers over a few of them. "May I?" he asked.

"Sure," Amelia replied.

He picked up one of the rabbits and rotated it. He tilted his head, rubbed his neck thoughtfully. "Graceful," he said simply as he replaced the rabbit. "Amelia, these are wonderful."

She liked the feeling that swept through her.

And she liked that her father didn't ask any questions when Louise handed her an envelope from Casey.

"He gave this to me when I saw him last night," said Louise. "He wanted you to have it."

"Thanks," said Amelia. "He's really okay?"

"He's okay. And remember, he's not too far away—about forty-five minutes. You'll see him again."

There was an awkward silence. Amelia

shifted her weight from foot to foot, flexed her toes. She felt clumsy. She turned the envelope in her hand. It said *Private*. The envelope was too big to put in her pocket, unless she folded it. She held it tightly and close, the word *Private* against her jacket, hidden.

"Well, thank you, Louise," her father said. "And thank you, Amelia, for showing me your beautiful creations. Okay. Let's go."

He wasn't one for lingering in situations like this.

As they walked out the door, he said, "I could use some coffee. Let's stop at the coffee shop. What do you say?"

"I say yes."

"Let's drink to human frailty," he said with a little laugh, "and, of course, its connection to love."

34 · POSTCARD

They sat at the window, exactly where Amelia had sat before with Casey. Sunlight streamed in, drawing attention to the array of crumbs on the tabletop.

"Too bright for you?" her father asked.

"No, I like it."

He swept the crumbs away with the side of his hand. "There," he said. "Much better."

The sun was warm and it felt good to her. She closed her eyes and lifted her head for a moment and imagined light seeping through her body.

He had coffee and she had hot chocolate.

They shared a molasses cookie the size of a saucer.

"Not as good as Mrs. O'Brien's," he said.

"Nothing is."

He cleared his throat. "Oh, before I forget . . ." He reached for the inside pocket of his sport coat, pulled something out, and passed it to her. "For you," he said. "I know you know about this."

It was the Babar postcard Hannah had told her about. Babar was lying in a bathtub, washing himself with a sponge. The postcard was yellowed and curled. The corners were worn, one was missing.

Amelia felt swimmy all of a sudden, for just a second. She had a vague memory of seeing the postcard before. She supposed it was a fragment of the movie of her life. A blurry part of her story from long, long ago.

"You never told me about this," said Amelia.

"You're right. I'm sorry. I guess there's a lot I haven't told. Haven't said. Haven't asked."

Amelia glanced downward. She'd hidden the envelope from Casey under her thigh. She pulled it out and put it on the table with the postcard. She waited for him to ask about it.

But he didn't.

And she didn't tell.

Maybe, she thought, I'm more like him than I admit. There were things she didn't talk about, too.

But there was something she wanted to ask. "When will I see Hannah again?"

His mouth drew down at the corners. "Would you like that?" he asked.

She nodded.

"Good," he said. "Soon. Soon and often, I hope."

"Me, too."

"This is a good window for watching

173

people," he said, changing the subject. Then he seemed to relax. He sipped his coffee, broke off another piece of the cookie, and ate it. In the bright sunshine, his freckled fingers looked pale, his knuckles wrinkled and baggy.

"Yeah." It was the perfect opening for her to tell him about Casey and naming people and Epiphany. Epiphany, the ghost mother. But she couldn't do it. She worried that it would bewilder him, or worse, make him cross.

But she could imagine telling Hannah about it someday. She could see Hannah finding the fantasy, the whole misunderstanding, interesting, logical, even touching. In her mind she could hear Hannah say: *While I was looking for you, you were looking for me. That's amazing!*

Amelia decided to be bold. "Want to play a game?" she asked.

"Huh?" He was squinting out the window.

"A game. Where you come up with stories for people. And give them names."

"I'm not very good at games," he said.

She drew up her shoulders, puckered her lips. "Oh, okay," she whispered.

Neither spoke. Amelia felt as if they were waiting for something. A few people hurried by outside. A striped cat crept down the sidewalk. A bird swooped dangerously close to the window.

And then Amelia saw her. Lindy Tussler—Feather—was walking past, looking determined, focused on something in the distance.

"I never liked that kid," her father said. He stiffened.

"What?"

"Lindy. I was glad when she was out of your life. I thought she was a miserable soul."

Amelia had never spoken a word to her father about Lindy Tussler and the end of their friendship. He never seemed curious about the details of her life. She never would have believed that he had an opinion about Lindy. *He knows more than I give him credit for,* she thought.

He leaned over and pushed the last bit of cookie toward her. "If I were playing your game, I'd call her Trouble."

Amelia's eyes widened. She looked up at her father. She burst out laughing.

He laughed, too.

Then they sat together quietly for a few more minutes before leaving. She felt something— the sounds of the coffee shop, the sunshine, the air—move in, settle, close gently around them.

35 · NEEDED

Amelia had wrapped the postcard in a napkin from the coffee shop and carefully put it in her jacket pocket for the walk home. She carried the envelope from Casey, switching it from hand to hand. She'd been clutching the envelope so tightly that it was wrinkled and warped by the time they got to their house.

She went right to her room and closed the door. She propped the postcard against the lamp on her nightstand. Then she sat on her bed and opened the envelope. There was a letter inside.

Dear Amelia,

Remember me?

Here's the news from one day after you saw me: My parents are getting legally separated. But I get to live in our house all the time. They promised that I don't have to move. They'll take turns staying here. Maybe I can trick myself into thinking we're still one big happy family. HA! But, at least, they're not divorced yet.

Starting next week I'll be coming to the clay studio on Saturdays. My aunt asked me. I can work (and get paid) or just make things (and smash them). HA!

How's Epiphany? I already forgot her real name. Sorry. I was kind of overwhelmed when you told me.

Do you remember that heart I made? I have to tell you something about it.

Signing off . . .

Casey

Amelia wondered what Casey would say about the heart. She'd seen what he'd carved into it: $C + A$. And she had the piece with the A on it as proof. Would he tell her that the A stood for *Amelia*? Would he tell her he liked her? She'd have to wait until next week to find out.

Although this was not the spring break she'd wanted, she wouldn't change it. It was funny how things worked out the way they did. If she had talked her father into taking her to Florida, her life would be very different right now.

She wouldn't have met Casey. She wouldn't have laughed, actually laughed, with her father in the coffee shop. And what about Hannah? And the Epiphany drama? And her show?

Amelia replaced the letter in the envelope. She tucked it and the postcard into her top dresser drawer with her letter from Natalie, the piece of Casey's heart, and the elastic band with the blue bead from Hannah.

She stood before the open drawer. She'd acquired these things in the last couple of days. Her little, hidden spring-break shrine. She touched the blue bead on the elastic band, then plucked the band from the drawer and crossed the room to the mirror on the back of her door. She ran her fingers through her hair—pulling, raking, gathering the long strands into a bun.

It wasn't perfect by any means—it was slightly lopsided—but it looked okay. "Poor thing," she whispered. She smiled at herself. No, I'm not, she thought. Not me. She lifted her chin. She turned her head from side to side. She chewed her lower lip. Then she peered at her reflected image straight on for a long time. She thought about the women in her life. Her mother, Mrs. O'Brien, Louise, Epiphany, Hannah. She knew it was strange, but she thought of Epiphany and Hannah as two different people.

She wondered what kind of woman she would be when she grew up.

Suddenly she worked the band out of her hair and shook her head. Her hair fell around her face and over her shoulders like a curtain. She went back to her dresser, returned the elastic band, and shut the drawer.

There was nothing of her mother's in her shrine, her drawer. Many years ago her father told her that he had a box of things that had belonged to her mother. The box was Amelia's; she just had to ask for it. She rarely thought about it. And she had never asked because he was hard to ask things of. And so much time had passed since he'd first told her about it. It had been so long ago that it was part of the lore of her childhood as she remembered it. But had she remembered it correctly? Besides, asking anything about her mother seemed to drop a weight of sadness on him that he carried around for hours or even days. But now, she thought she could ask. She would.

There was nothing of Mrs. O'Brien's in her shrine, either. But there were things from Mrs. O'Brien everywhere. From the curtains in Amelia's room to her bedspread to her lacy pillowcases to her favorite necklace to bracelets. On and on and on. And Mrs. O'Brien, herself, was there, always there, day after day.

Amelia wondered what would happen to Mrs. O'Brien if Hannah stayed in her father's life. She hated to consider certain possibilities. But, no matter what, Mrs. O'Brien would be right across the street.

Did she hear Mrs. O'Brien?

Amelia left her room and wandered down the hall, listening. As if she somehow knew she was being thought of, Mrs. O'Brien called out in a cheerful voice. "Amelia? I'm in the kitchen. I need you."

No, thought Amelia. I need you.

She needed her to sweep her up, to hold her close, to understand her, to love her. She needed her to tell her when she didn't need her anymore.

"Coming," Amelia called back.

When she grabbed the banister, she took a deep breath. Let it out. She was ready. She didn't want to keep Mrs. O'Brien waiting. She brightened as she quickly and quietly descended the stairs—into the kitchen, into the world, into whatever was still to come.